About *The Below*

When hard-nosed lawyer Beth follows a strange man into a hidden cave, she finds herself in a massive subterranean world known as "The Below". As she learns about this secret place and grows closer to her guide, she discovers a surprising side to herself. But all is not as it seems in The Below, and the apparent tranquility of the path she treads may obscure a darker truth. **The Below** is a novella about change, purpose, and self-discovery.

Other Books

The Tale of Rin: Protege (*novel*): Just because Rin is indestructible doesn't mean she can't be hurt. On her quest to remedy an ancient sin, a single act of casual cruelty sets off an avalanche of events which threaten to destroy everything. Rin must rein in her assistant, a man of fierce attachment and questionable conviction, while avoiding a devious ex-husband who will stop at nothing to reclaim her. In the balance lies her heart and the fate of the world.

PACE (*novel*): A mysterious Front, originating in Scotland and slowly expanding outward, threatens humanity's existence. In defiance of the known laws of physics, it only kills humans and is otherwise undetectable. Panic-stricken nations struggle against both the advancing menace and a tide of civil unrest. Desperate individuals must find their own paths and find them quickly. Mankind has only a few years to pool its rapidly dwindling resources and save itself from extinction.

The Delivery (*novella*): Wilbur is an unassuming little man living an unassuming little life. He and his wife have a stereotypical 1950s existence but in modern America. One day, he arrives home to discover a mysterious crate. His attempts to deal with it trigger an escalating series of absurdities that strain his marriage, leave the couple's life in tatters, and lead him to question his place in the world.

The Man Who Stands in Line (*flash fiction*): Killer flies, amorous dinosaurs, angry buildings, and one very large fish — all in a single volume. A surreal and humorous view of the usual questions of self, purpose, and society. This quirky collection of flash fiction, vignettes, and poetry is variously absurd, dark, and comic. *Also available as an audiobook.*

The Way Around (*flash fiction*): More absurd, horrifying, and downright inexplicable shorts. Included are such soon-to-be classics as Buzz-Saw Bob, the sport of pendulum watching, yet another secret to ultimate success, the art of gasping, a neighbor who is definitely not Mr. Rogers, and Buddha's morning commute. *Also available as an audiobook.*

The Last Cloud (*flash fiction*): Meet the superhero Spleen Squeezer, discover the true story of Eden, and travel to the safest city in the world in this 3rd collection of unclassifiable ultra-short pieces. But wait, there's MORE!!!! Learn the danger of having ears, the importance of being unlikable, and how to achieve quality as an executioner. *Also available as an audiobook.*

*All are available as **paperbacks** through **Amazon**, **Barnes & Noble**, **Waterstones**, and other bookstores in the U.S. and internationally, as **Kindle ebooks** through **Amazon**, and (where applicable) as **audiobooks** through **Audible**.*

The Below

THE BELOW

by

K.M. Halpern

Ɛpsilon Books

Copyright © 2023 by K.M. Halpern

All rights reserved.

ISBN-13 (paperback): 978-1-945671-17-3

ISBN-13 (ebook): 978-1-945671-18-0

Library of Congress Control Number: 2023917732

Published by Epsilon Books

Printed in the United States of America

First Edition

DISCLAIMER: This is a work of fiction. If it weren't, we all would have much bigger problems than worrying about who wrote what about whom. Nonetheless, since it seems obligatory to state the obvious, any resemblance of characters in this work to real individuals, living or deceased, is purely coincidental.

The Below

The Rottweilers were new. They hadn't been here the last time he emerged in this area.

As always, the opening blended almost imperceptibly into its surroundings — this time the field behind a cul-de-sac. He never was sure how it appeared to others, but the dogs gave him a clue.

As he snaked through the grass on his belly, he spotted a house nearby, a warm glow in the looming dusk. Two women, young. Maybe not so young. Too far to tell. Then the Rottweilers.

The animals themselves weren't a problem, but they did make things awkward. He didn't like having his egresses noticed and would have forgone them altogether if possible, but it was important to emerge from time to time for reasons he could not remember or maybe never knew.

Lately, he had found it harder to muster the energy to do so. His excursions above had grown short and infrequent, but that didn't mean he had forgotten how to handle himself. He turned and crawled back toward the opening.

His biggest concern was that the dogs would follow him too far. The way normally was closed to them, or maybe they simply could not perceive it. Following him was one way to get in, but if they intruded too far they would never find their way back out. That would be unfair to them. It wasn't their fault that they were doing what dogs were supposed to do.

He retreated through the cavernous tunnel until he found a convenient spot, still somewhat green but now lightly forested. This would do. He picked up a stick and stood his ground. The first dog launched itself at his arm, but its teeth found only wood. Its companion stood barking but made no move to interfere. For some reason they never did. There was something about the place which confounded animals. Not enough to deter them from following, but enough to disorient them when they did. Dogs ordinarily found strength in packs. That was their advantage. But not here. Here they had no advantage. Of course, it did not really matter. Alone or together, they could not harm him. Not on *his* ground. Or possibly any other, though he was unsure.

The dog's vicious mauling of the stick began to abate. It was an old trick, one which only worked below. He was unsure *why* it worked, but it did. Once a dog had the stick, its attention never transferred to him. Perhaps a dog's mind could not encompass more than one target. Its animosity attached to the stick, then slowly dissipated. The stick was dead. That was its goal, and its companion's as well. Submission and death. The dogs' duty done, they now were bereft of purpose. No longer hostile, they gently sauntered up to him, panting. He pet each in turn.

"They're not supposed to do that."

The female voice issued from the dark of the tunnel, echoing in all the wrong places. It did not surprise him. The dogs had followed, and their masters could too. He had been aware of such an eventuality before he emerged. It was one of the dangers of doing so. Was that *why* he emerged?

It and its companion. Like the dogs, there were two. This he could sense long before their forms were visible. One woman seemed less tangible than the other, or perhaps less consequential. The dogs were unambiguously there, unambiguously equal. Why was it different for their owners? He easily could forget the second woman and made an effort not to. She certainly would become lost in this place. Though perhaps less faultless than the dogs, she too was following her nature and did not deserve such a fate.

He bore the women no ill will. Though less pliable than dogs, these creatures could be reasoned with. He would convince them to return home, to forget. Just like the others. He could be very persuasive in this place.

Instead, he found himself conversing lightly with the women. It had been a long time, but he did not feel rusty. One was blonde and young, maybe in her early twenties. The other was somewhat older. Late twenties, early thirties? It did not matter. He now was certain that one of them had drawn him to the surface, though he remained unsure which. Just because one woman seemed less consequential did not mean she *was* less consequential.

Before he realized it, he found himself on the lawn by the house. He breathed a sigh of relief. Though he did not recall how, he must have spoken the right words to lead them out. He wondered if they could retrace their way in. Perhaps they had an organ to accomplish this, unlike the dogs. If so, none of the others had used it.

He looked down. The younger woman was offering him something.

"Would you like the key?"

He shook his head. It was smaller and less grand than the keys he was accustomed to, but this was not the reason he refused.

"Thank you, but I do not need one," he explained.

"Really, it's no trouble," the older woman replied. "This is our mother's house, but she fell ill while away and is in a hospital on the other side of the country."

"I see."

"We stopped by to look in on her home. You would be doing us a favor since we don't know how long she will be away," the younger one insisted, pressing the oddly shaped key into his hand.

He did not know why, but they always offered keys. He had no need of such things, but there was no way to make them understand that. He already had access to far too many places. A key carried responsibility. If everyone could access a place, nobody was responsible for it. But if only a few could, the whole burden of its existence lay with them.

Was that why she insisted? Maybe it was her way of seeking to bind him. If so, she was mistaken in this — but it would be impolite to tell her this.

With a nod, he accepted the key. It would do no harm to grant them this, for he had no intention of returning here. The women seemed grateful but on the verge of tears.

"Is her condition grave?" he asked.

The younger woman tried to put on a brave face but could not manage it.

"Why do you not go to her, then?" he asked.

The women seemed puzzled for a moment, and he wondered whether they took his suggestion for a reproach.

"We can't," the older sister explained. "The way still is not passable. We will have to wait until things improve."

He sighed. Such tragedy was part and parcel of the farce of the surface, and he would be relieved when free of it once more. He resolved not to emerge again for a long time, perhaps ever. If he did, it would be far from this place.

"I can take you there," he offered before he was aware of it. "If you wish."

The younger sister seemed doubtful, almost afraid. The older did not hesitate.

"Please." She took his hand in hers and looked him in the eyes. "It would mean a lot."

"Then let us go."

The woman waved at her sister, who stood by the house and watched in stunned silence as she followed him down the tunnel.

"What if my sister changes her mind?" the woman asked. "Will she be able to catch up to us?"

He shook his head. "She will not change her mind."

The woman followed in silence, as the tunnel passed through vegetation, then dirt, then concrete. Graffiti appeared but quickly tapered off. At times the tunnel had the immaculate appearance of a conduit, at others it resembled a grassy ravine. There always was sufficient light, though she could not tell from where.

"I'm Beth," she ventured after they had traveled some distance.

"So you are."

"What's your name?" She sounded chipper, almost nervous.

He thought for a few moments. "Rake. I think it is Rake."

"That is an odd name."

"Maybe."

"So, where are you from Rake?"

"Here and there."

"Originally?"

Rake stopped and looked at her. He pointed up.

After that, they walked in silence.

Beth wasn't sure how long they had been walking or what she had been thinking about the whole time. Their surroundings had changed gradually, almost imperceptibly. The tunnel currently took the form of a narrow canal but was obstructed ahead. Her heart began to race. What would happen now?

"Is this the end?" she asked.

Rake shook his head. "This is the beginning."

He stepped over some rubble and offered her his hand. With trepidation, she took it. His grip was strong, but the hand itself felt delicate, almost paper-like. She wanted to poke Rake to see what would happen but feared he would burst. She did not want to be alone.

"Stay close," he warned. "It is easy to get lost. Many have."

Beth shuddered at the thought. Had those people wandered in by accident? She wanted to ask what had happened to them, but that would have to wait. If she did not wish to join their number she needed to focus on keeping up with Rake.

Picking her way over the rubble, Beth now saw where he was leading her. What had appeared to be the end of the tunnel actually was a vast wall. It extended as far as she could see in every direction, though she wondered how she could see so far in the dim light. And how could the wall be so tall? She did not think they had descended that much. To their left, obscured by the rubble, was a small gap from which light emanated.

Rake ushered her through it. Turning, she was relieved to find the opening still there, though the dark mirror of before. It was distinctly less inviting from this side.

Beth's eyes took some time to adjust to the strong light. When they did, she was surprised by her surroundings. She was in a basement of some sort, with a concrete cellar floor, a light industrial rug, a pool table, and a few fabric chairs, well-worn. The walls were made of cheap wood paneling.

"Is this your place?" she asked.

"It is a place."

Rake motioned her to follow. Passing through a door, they emerged into a long thin space, made thinner by crowded metal shelves along the sides. Another door led to an oddly misshapen room filled with poorly stacked books. Through several open doors, she caught glimpses of other rooms too dark to discern.

Rake guided her toward one such door, and they passed into another room and then another. Each was well-enough lit to navigate comfortably, but most appeared dim from outside. However, it wasn't as if a light switched on when she and Rake entered. Beth decided the illumination must be directional.

Or maybe it followed Rake, though he did not carry a torch of any sort. This occasioned a brief panic. If she was not with him, would this place be pitch black? What would emerge from that dark? For some reason, she was less afraid of being along in the dark than she would have imagined. She was unsure whether this was because the prospect did not seem likely or did not seem so bad.

"Why are you doing this for me?" Beth asked.

They were passing through the rusting carapace of some old waterworks. Huge pipes, mostly cracked, loomed overhead and shadowed the path. She and Rake even had crawled through one for a short stint. She would have guessed that an old, crumbling pipe could only lead to a few places, none of them good. To her surprise, they had emerged into a bright, shiny kitchen. She got the distinct impression that it had not been used in some time, or perhaps ever. What purpose could a kitchen serve in this place?

"I'm not sure," Rake replied, disrupting her reverie. "It felt like the right thing to do."

Beth eyed him skeptically. "It's an awfully big favor."

"Not necessarily."

"Do you have an ulterior motive? Something sinister?" She was half joking, but half was a smaller fraction than she would have preferred.

"I would have walked this path sooner or later, so why not walk it now with you?"

She looked at him. "Well, thank you. Whatever your reason, it means a lot to me."

Rake thought for a moment. "I think someone did the same for me, once."

"You have a sick mother?"

"I have a mother. I had a mother."

"I'm sorry," Beth offered.

"There is no need. You did nothing to her."

"I mean, my condolences." Was he purposely misconstruing her or was it genuine? Maybe he was being contrarian.

"She is not dead, I think. I just do not know where she is."

Beth gasped. "She's lost? In here?!?"

Before Rake could reply, she clutched his arm. "Is that why you wander around down here?"

"She is not lost. I simply do not know where she

is. Or if she still is at all."

This sounded terribly callous to Beth, and she looked at Rake anew. What sort of person was he really? What was he doing down here? Why was he leading her through ... whatever this was? She had followed a complete stranger into a hole in the ground. He could do anything to her, and nobody would stop him. Nobody would know.

Beth felt her pulse. It had not risen at all. However strongly she voiced these fears to herself, they failed to take root. Despite her best efforts to recast Rake in a sinister light, she could not.

This was new and profoundly disconcerting to her. Recasting people in a sinister light was what Beth did best. Professionally, it was her bread and butter, and she applied these talents as liberally to her personal life as her professional one. Nobody was spared, including her sister.

Nor was it a difficult task in this case. Even setting aside their questionable surroundings, Rake's replies alone should have been cause for concern. Language was inherently ambiguous, and everything Rake said doubly so. She replayed his words and tried to read into them threats and derision and innuendo, but could not. Something allayed these worries. Something told her it would be okay. It was proving impossible to create a tower of villainy for him.

Beth realized she trusted the man. Could it really be that simple? This felt particularly ironic. The woman who trusted nobody had decided to completely trust a stranger. And not any stranger, but a stranger of the creepiest sort. Had she no instinct for self-preservation? Had he *done* something to her? Perhaps he'd slipped her a drug. What other explanation could there be? Even this suspicion found no purchase. Any edifice Beth tried to erect melted like butter before it could take form.

"Don't you miss her?" she asked after a few minutes of such reequilibration. She tried not to sound judgmental.

"I do not remember her."

Beth relaxed. So, that was it. A perfectly innocent explanation. His mother left when he was very young. If they never had time to develop a bond, the boy would not miss his mother. At most, he would miss the idea of her. Beth wondered why this justification was so important. Why did it matter whether the guy was a selfish prick? Most men were.

Despite herself, she was pleased with her newfound equanimity. If this was the doing of a drug, Beth wished she'd discovered it long ago. How many past relationships had she lost (or never had) without the benefit of such a palliative? Would its magic cease when she returned to the surface? She hoped to remain this way, and promised herself to try. Maybe not quite *this* serene, but more than she had been. Beth wished she could record how she felt now, for easy recall when needed. She resolved to attend more closely to the mechanisms of her mood.

"Did you ever try to find her?" she asked. She doubted there was a way to phrase this which wouldn't sound judgmental, and didn't bother to try.

If her question bothered him, Rake did not show it. Beth couldn't explain why, but she really wanted to fluster the man. Not anger him, just penetrate the vaguely detached air he exuded.

"I do not know where to look," he replied at length. "The world is a big place."

Beth looked up at him. "I tell you what. After we attend to my mother, I'll help you find yours." She thought for a second, then smiled. "If you wish."

Rake smiled back. It was the first smile she had seen, a smile which could have meant anything.

By now, they had arrived at a sprawling network of tiled rooms. It reminded her loosely of a park restroom facility, but was more elaborate than any she had encountered. One room had an open shower area and another had benches, perhaps for a sauna. She had never been to a public bathhouse, but decided this must be what one looked like.

When they entered the first room, which closely resembled a public urinal, Beth tied her hair back. Who knew what sort of grime it could brush against in here? To her relief, there were no dubious stains on the porcelain or floor. Everything was white, but faded rather than sparkling. The dullness of the finish was too uniform to come from overuse. It felt like the tarnish of having never been used. Were the fixtures born dull, or had they aged into it? There was no sun down here to bleach them. Maybe some sort of chemical process was at work.

"You need not worry," Rake said. "Go if you need to."

Beth looked around with an air of distaste. "No thanks. I'm fine."

She realized that she *was* fine. Why didn't she have to go? They had been walking for hours, but Beth felt no need to relieve herself. Was she dehydrated? That raised another issue, one she was surprised had not occurred to her before.

"Is there food or water down here?" she asked.

Rake looked at her. "Are you hungry or thirsty?"

Beth shook her head.

"Let me know if you are, and we'll find something."

This didn't sound very convincing, but she decided to drop the matter. It wasn't presently an issue, and she could raise it again when it became one.

Besides, there had to be *something* in this cave. Otherwise, how did Rake get by? *Was* this a cave? She had been walking with Rake for quite a while but still had no idea what the place was. Things seemed a lot less damp and moldy than she would have expected from a cave. They were underground, but it didn't feel particularly subterranean. More like a basement or an old dwelling. Would a basement have food? Maybe there was a pantry somewhere. They *had* seen a kitchen. It stood to reason there would be a place to stock it.

How *did* Rake get by? Beth wondered how long he had been in this place, traversing these tunnels. Could he do so if the light failed? How had it *not* failed? She had so many questions but hesitated to pepper him with them. Somehow she knew that his answers, however well-intentioned, would only serve to confuse her more.

"Do you live down here?" Beth finally asked, some time during what she assumed was the second day of their journey. By now, she had gotten used to the oddly tortuous path. In some places it felt like a musty basement, in others an abandoned subway tunnel. They even had crossed a few wooded areas, though she saw no wildlife and it was hard to tell the color of the trees. Everything seemed distorted, though she could not pinpoint precisely how.

One thing that had become clear was that they were traversing defined spaces, or at least that is what Rake called them. The boundaries sometimes were obvious, other times less so. A subtle shift in lighting could be the only clue that they had crossed into a new space, but most of the time there was a distinct threshold. It usually wasn't as pronounced as the transition between rooms in a house or between inside and outside — though sometimes that's precisely what it was. More often, it felt like moving between different rooms in different houses, maybe even different lands. Different worlds? Beth doubted it was anything so extraordinary. She suspected there was a mundane explanation for all this and that she would be terribly disappointed to learn it.

Most of the spaces had multiple exits, or perhaps entrances. That was another thing Beth was uncertain of. Rake once had hinted that the two were not the same. Common sense told her that every exit also was an entrance, but common sense did not always apply down here. Was there a prescribed order in which the spaces had to be traversed? Maybe the path was irreversible, and no trail of breadcrumbs could guide her back. Rake also had said that people got lost. Was that how?

She wondered whether they were the sort of people who *would* get lost. Perhaps they were the type who always knew where they were and where they were going. Always, but not here. Beth decided it was irrelevant what "type" they were. Lost was lost. It did not matter how one got lost. Once lost, a person would never be found. Not down here. Not if the dark closed in. Once again the thought should have terrified her, and once again it did not.

Beth looked around. They appeared to be in some sort of chapel. She watched as Rake quietly picked his way past obstacles and selected one of the five doorways without hesitation. No, she was thinking about this wrong. However strange it seemed, this was a defined place with defined ways. She just didn't know the definitions. There had to be a method, some way to stick to the path and know where it went. If so, it continued to elude her.

Rake always seemed to know which way to go. Did he remember the path or make his own? For a while Beth had tried to discern some pattern in how he chose which threshold to cross and which space to enter, but she gave up after the first day. He somehow just knew, or at least she prayed he did. Beth refused to ask him directly. It would be dangerous to ask such a question. He could answer it.

"Do you live down here?" she repeated. Had he not heard her the first time? Maybe her thoughts were loud enough to drown out the question. Had she actually asked it?

Rake shrugged. "I live and I am here, so you could say that."

Beth rolled her eyes from habit but felt no annoyance.

"Are you trapped down here?" she clarified.

He gave her a puzzled look. "We met above."

"But maybe you are bound to this place somehow."

Rake shook his head. "I do not think so. I can go above when I wish. I used to often," — his forehead furrowed for a moment as he tried to recall something — "but then less so."

"You went above less, or you wished to go above less?"

"The two are the same. Why would I do something I do not wish or wish for something I cannot do?" He smiled and tapped her forehead. "Do you do things you do not wish or wish for things you cannot do?"

Beth gave an awkward grin. "Almost exclusively."

"Perhaps it has to do with being above? There are things which do not make sense above, but maybe that only is by the logic below. The opposite may be true too. Do the things down here make sense to you?"

Beth was hesitant to answer that. The things down here *did* make sense, and she was bothered by this. Had she become acclimated to the place? Maybe it had assimilated her.

"I do not understand the above," Rake

announced. "I never did, even when I lived there."

Beth felt an inexplicable need to defend her home. "Maybe it is better now."

He gave her a pointed look. "It would seem not."

Beth smiled and took his hand in hers. "It's not so bad. Maybe I can show you around sometime, like you're doing for me down here."

"Is that what I am doing? I thought we were going somewhere."

Beth gave a shy grin. "I think we are, but it's too early to tell."

He said nothing, and she sighed.

"When were you last up there?" she asked after a minute of awkward silence.

"You saw me."

"Before then."

"It has been a while."

"Then that is why," Beth replied.

"Why what?"

Beth waved at the room. "Everything looks so old-fashioned."

"I see. So the world has changed above."

Beth stared at him. "You saw our house, our lawn, our dogs. And I'm so sorry about sic'ing them on you. We were startled."

"It is no matter. The house and the lawn and the dogs did not seem dissimilar from other houses and lawns and dogs. But it is hard to be sure. That the outsides of houses and lawns and dogs look the same does not mean they *are* the same."

As if in keeping with their conversation, the scenery changed.

Rake stopped. "This place is different. I do not remember it."

"You've lost your way?" This should have inspired panic, but instead Beth felt relief. If he could lose his way, it meant he was fallible. That made him seem more human, more accessible.

"It is the right room, but the room is wrong."

At first, Beth had tried to memorize their path in case she needed to retrace it. However, she quickly had given up, and the spaces they traversed had long since blurred. She could barely recall most of them. For the first time in many hours, she attended closely to her surroundings.

"It looks ... normal," Beth gasped. Did this mean they were getting closer to the surface? Perhaps the arc of their journey was nearing its end. She recognized the sensation from hiking, which did not bode well. What felt like the final mile inevitably turned out to be several.

"Ah, this is how you see the world," Rake replied.

"Will there be more spaces like this one? I thought the rooms all were old and stuffy."

Rake stopped walking, and Beth realized she may have insulted him.

"But charming in their own way," she quickly added.

He sniffed the air, apparently oblivious to her words. "It has changed."

"Because I'm here?"

"No, because *we* are here. We have traveled this path together for some time now. Such a thing has consequences. It is fundamentally different from traveling the same path at the same time separately."

We. The word pleased Beth. Was she meant to read it this way? With Rake it was hard to tell anything, which made her wonder all the more why she *wanted* him to say such a thing. She was tempted to ask, to demand certainty. But she wasn't sure she wanted to know the answer, or which answer she wanted. She decided to change the subject.

"Will I be stuck down here?" she finally managed.

"Stuck?"

"Will I become like you?"

"How so?"

Beth suddenly grew awkward. "I'm sorry. I didn't mean to make that sound like a bad thing."

"You gave no offense. I do not know what I look like, so I cannot tell you whether you will become like me. Perhaps you started that way."

Beth could not suppress a giggle at this. When was the last time she had *giggled*? What was she — twelve? She turned beet red and wished the ground would swallow her. She closed her eyes and desperately hoped Rake hadn't noticed.

"How can you *not* know what you look like?" she asked in an obvious attempt to divert his attention.

"I never look at myself," he replied.

They continued in silence for another hour before Beth finally saw the item she was looking for. It was sitting on a side shelf of a strange little room whose purpose she could not surmise. But that purpose was irrelevant; she had what she wanted.

Beth held up the hand mirror.

"Ah, that is how I look," Rake murmured. He

stooped and surveyed his features. "I am more beautiful than I imagined."

Beth smiled. "And modest. There are mirrors around, so why don't you ever look in one?"

"A mirror I hold would show how I look to me. A mirror you hold shows how I look to you."

Beth turned a deep crimson.

"How do you look to you?" she asked after a minute.

"Like me."

She pushed the mirror at him. "Here, hold it. I want to see how you look to you."

He shook his head. "What good would that do? Each person sees another differently. The way you see that person encompasses everything which matters to you. Anything more would merely serve to muddle things."

She grinned. "Let's muddle things."

Rake smiled and quietly replaced the mirror on its shelf. "Best not to. It is impolite to inquire too closely into the conceits of others."

After several more minutes, Beth finally mustered the courage to ask the question which had been gnawing at her.

"How do I look to you?"

"Does it matter how you appear to another?"

She stopped and looked at him. "Not another. You."

"I am not you, so I am another."

"Am I beautiful?" she demanded. If blunt was needed, blunt she would be.

"You are the one I invited to travel with me, and you are the one who accepted that invitation."

Beth's face sank. "That's a nice way of saying I am not beautiful to you." She had expected him to dodge the question, but had not expected it to rankle so much.

Rake gave her a quiet look. "It is not that you are not beautiful to me. It is that such things have no meaning here."

Beth felt her temper rise. Why did every answer have to be an exercise in obfuscation? His words were as labyrinthine as the place itself.

"Why does it matter if we are down here or up above? It's just you and me," she blurted out, immediately regretting her tone. He did not seem to notice.

"It matters," came the inevitable reply.

Rake said nothing for the next few minutes, and Beth followed in silence until they reached a space with a bench. She plopped down on it. As always, he somehow sensed that she had stopped. When he turned to see why, she gave him puppy eyes. Beth was sure that this sort of nonsense never worked outside the movies — and it certainly wouldn't work for *her* on *him*.

To her surprise, he sat next to her. She couldn't tell whether he understood *what* bothered her or simply that something did. Would he manage to figure out what she wanted to hear? The man seemed awfully obtuse when it came to certain things. At least, she hoped he just was being obtuse.

Rake looked like he was preparing to say something. Anything which required preparation was bound to be something she did not want to hear. She expected a speech about their different backgrounds and the incompatibility of their worlds, a brushoff that wasn't quite a brushoff. Would the rest of their trip be an exercise in awkwardness? She knew she was being unreasonable. He was doing what he had promised, and she was the one demanding more. Beth braced herself.

"Things here are shadows of those above," Rake explained, "formed from them but distinct. They are separate and live their own lives, no longer bound to parent or principle. Are they more beautiful than their progenitors or less? When their parents cease to be, are they then more beautiful by dint of existence?"

His words drove home her utter inability to predict anything about the man. Was that what drew her to him?

"I don't understand," she complained. *Was* this some sort of rejection? Maybe it was the prelude to one. Damn the man, why couldn't he be direct? She didn't need a philosophical exegesis on why he was rejecting her.

His eyes were warm, almost sorrowful. "You will. There is no beauty or ugliness here. Only what is. The ideals which bind you to the world above have no sway here. There are no fetters. We only are constrained to the places and paths of this world, and these never grow tiresome."

Beth stared, transfixed, unsure whether she was looking at him or through him. He made it sound like this was its own world, something decoupled — or perhaps never coupled. And there *was* the small matter of not needing to eat or drink. That left two possibilities, three if she included the one she really did not wish to consider. She decided it was best to start with the most palatable alternative.

"Is this some sort of dream world? You're a dream guide, aren't you? Some sort of mystical mumbo-jumbo dream-guide. Of course, that would mean that I believe in mystical mumbo-jumbo or maybe want to since I'm the one dreaming and —"

"It is no dream world," Rake corrected, paying no mind to Beth's stream of babble or where he chose to ford it. Seeing the concern on her face, he added, "But I too can dream and sometimes do."

"You sleep?" Beth had not seen him do so. Maybe she hadn't noticed? If she perceived time differently here, maybe he slept between moments. Or, less poetically, on his feet. That would explain the long silences as he led. The prospect of a sleepwalking guide certainly wasn't a comforting one. It was also rather implausible.

Rake nodded. "When I am tired."

She could not envision Rake getting tired. Not in this place. Perhaps he meant that he dreamt above? Or maybe he slept when he wasn't guiding anyone. She imagined him as an inanimate object on one of the shelves, awakening now and then for an excursion above. Beth liked the idea of him being awake specifically for her.

"What do you dream of?" she wondered aloud. It was a silly question, and far from the most compelling she could think of. This was the sort of small talk she detested, but she could not help herself. Could anything be more boring than another person's dreams? They were of substance only to the dreamer, spoken in an internal language that had meaning to nobody else. It was like the incomprehensible gibberish of a child, and just as interesting.

Though ... maybe that wasn't true of Rake. She genuinely wondered what he *did* dream about, but that wasn't the real reason she asked. The question was a desperate attempt to distract herself from the obvious. If this was not a dream world, only two conceivable explanations remained, and she was one such possibility away from a truly alarming eventuality. Rake wasn't exactly the forthcoming type, but something warned her that he *would* answer when she least wanted him to.

"I dream of many things," he replied with a languid air. "The world above as it was. Sometimes as it should be. But never as it is."

Something occurred to Beth, and she wondered why it hadn't before. He *did* say that he used to live up above. For some reason, she associated Rake with this place through and through.

"Were you born above?" she asked.

Rake nodded. "I was. It may be possible to be born here, but I was not."

"How long ago?" Beth realized it was rude to ask his age but doubted he would offer it.

Rake shrugged. "Which number you call your age merely depends on how you choose to demarcate time."

Rather than invite another evasion, Beth took a different tack. "If you rarely go above, how do you know what it is like now?"

"You can see it around you."

"Maybe that's how it once was, but not anymore. I told you — this stuff is way out of date."

"This is how I wish to remember it."

Beth studied him. "So you *are* responsible for all this." She gestured openly at their surroundings.

He smiled. "I'd like to imagine I have a better imagination than this."

Beth looked around. The surroundings encompassed by her gesture included an old toilet, stored upside down, and a metal rack of record albums, arranged with casual disregard for their well-being. She gave a snort of irritation at finding her point sabotaged by happenstance and resolved to pay closer attention to her environs before speaking next time. This was a mistake she would *not* have made professionally. Instead, she would have artfully arranged for circumstances to favor whatever point she cared to make. In her experience, there was no less faithful friend than serendipity.

"I am not why it is this way," Rake clarified in the face of her silence. "That is a happy coincidence."

Was he enjoying this? That almost would make the blunder worth it. She had assumed early on that he was the sort of person who did not understand sarcasm, though in retrospect it was hard to pin down exactly why. Much about the man smacked of anachronism, and sarcasm itself was an anachronism from the age where direct insults could invite a fatal duel.

Maybe he was sarcastic all along, too subtle for his audience. Table for one, please. Beth often had felt that way herself. She would be acutely embarrassed if she was the fool in the room this time.

She wished she could recall all his exact words and accompanying facial expressions. It was hard to discern his facial expression when most of his words were cast over his shoulder, but something told her she would have no better luck if they were face to face the entire time.

Rake's eyes were on her, and Beth realized he expected a reply. Expected or desired? He would wait a polite length of time and then assume this latest bout of communication had concluded. Just like a robot. She had to think of something to say. Preferably something witty. What was it that he had said about imagination?

"If you could imagine your imagination, then wouldn't something come from nothing?" she blurted out.

"Something always comes from nothing, and imagination is no exception. If you cannot imagine imagination, then you certainly will not be able to imagine reality."

His reply came a bit too readily, as if it had been on the tip of his tongue. Beth had a hard time believing he was *that* quick on his feet, especially with nobody to practice on down here. Perhaps he had a repertoire of rehearsed answers. How many times had he done this? She liked to believe her questions and concerns were original, not tired variations of the very things her unnamed predecessors had pondered.

"You don't need to imagine reality," she objected. "You experience it."

"Not here. That is one advantage of this place."

Beth touched his arm. "Was it that bad?"

He looked at her and did not pull away. "You tell me."

"Me?" She was taken aback. Had she offended him somehow? Despite his gentle tone, it felt like he was flinging her comment back in her face. She withdrew her hand and immediately regretted it. He finally was opening up to her, if in his own way. Maybe.

"I still live above," she replied. "I never said it was bad."

Rake shrugged. "You are the one who showed no fear. You are the one traveling with me."

"That was just..." She stopped, unable to explain it to him any more than to herself.

"Are you trying to find something or escape something?" he asked. "It always is one of those two." The question had a rhetorical quality, yet felt like a reproach. But a reproach for what? He had offered and she had accepted. Was there anything wrong with that?

They walked in silence for some time before Beth said anything. It was not an uncomfortable silence, and she did not feel the need to break it as she had the previous day. Day? Had it been a day? Days? Maybe weeks? She had lost all track of time. The dim light gave no clue, and she was sure any clock she found down here would not be trustworthy. Clocks that old would not know how to tell modern time.

They were from an era when time did not matter as much or move as fast.

When she finally spoke, it was because a thought had been forming in her mind for a while, a thought which now demanded recognition.

"I haven't seen anyone else since we came down here," she observed. "There are things, and what you call spaces, but nothing living. Not even a bird."

"Did you expect to find birds deep beneath the ground?"

"Deep?" Beth didn't feel like they had descended that far, though perhaps the path had an imperceptible grade. She would have expected the air to feel close and stifling deep beneath the ground, but instead it seemed in keeping with her surroundings. The scents were what she would expect of each space, though never unpleasant. She wondered if the bacteria or molds responsible for unpleasant odors could survive down here.

If Beth had suddenly awoken in any of the spaces so far, she would not have guessed they were deep beneath the surface. However, she did not mistrust Rake on this point. He had no reason to lie. If he did not know, he would have said so. Or, more likely, he would have confused the issue with some mushy platitude.

All this begged the question of what precisely he meant by "deep". That word could be interpreted quite differently by different people.

"How deep would you say we are?" she ventured after a few minutes.

"We are as deep as we are."

Ah, the obligatory tautology. Or was that his way

of telling her to shut up and stop bothering him? It felt like the sort of reflexive response one may offer a pestering child. Beth sighed. She gave the man too much credit. Maybe he actually *didn't* know. Once again, she felt an overwhelming desire to discomfit him.

She pouted. "If you don't know, just say so."

"There is above and there is below, everything else is an irrelevant matter of degree." There was no testiness in his voice, but she wondered if he felt some. Flustering him was different from irritating him, and she had no desire to do the latter.

"Caves usually have critters," she pointed out, reverting to her earlier concern. "Bats, maybe rats."

"Would you prefer to see some rats?"

Beth imagined a torrent of ravenous vermin pouring in from all sides, something from a horror movie. Did such things actually happen in these places? It seemed plausible. What about bugs? There had to be bugs. Didn't most of them live underground? Such a large subterranean space should be filled with bugs. She was about to ask but stopped herself. This definitely was one of those questions she *didn't* want to know the answer to.

She gave an instinctive shudder, but felt nothing. No revulsion, no fear, no hope. The image of the bugs remained a mere image and had no hold on her. If swarmed, she would experience the thing with detachment — at least until the first wet bite cured her of such indifference. Even that prospect did not worry her. She suspected she would sense when such a specter was real — or about to become real. Was there a difference?

⁓•⁓

After a long spell ruminating on such things, Beth realized the most important question remained unasked. The original question.

"Fine, forget the birds," she began.

"They are absent but not forgotten."

Beth gave him a bemused look. "Where are the people? You're a person, so I'm sure there must be others."

She was anything *but* sure, and hoped he would be more apt to correct a misconception than answer an outright question. She had used such a tactic in the past professionally, with some success.

Rake did not turn or stop. "They are not sociable."

The way he said this unsettled her more than anything so far. She still felt no fear, only a vague disquiet. Would he protect her, and from what exactly?

"Are we safe?"

"What does it mean to be safe?"

His words irritated her more than usual. Was he deliberately evading her questions, or was he actually this heedless? She needed him not to be heedless. He was all that stood between her and spending the rest of her days lost in this catacomb. Or worse.

"It means what it sounds like," Beth replied with some heat. "Are we in danger from this ... stuff? From these places? Are there things here which can hurt us?"

Rake stopped and looked around. He picked up a hammer from a nearby table, and Beth had the horrible premonition he was going to strike her. Was this the logical conclusion to her story? She often had suspected her life was heading for this sort of ending. Would any other be satisfactory?

Rake tapped his own arm so gently that Beth barely heard a sound. A brownish-blue patch quickly formed under his skin. Did bruises usually appear so quickly? And how had such a gentle tap done this? The man was either very strong or very fragile.

"Are you okay?" she asked, grabbing his arm.

"Why would I not be?"

"Because you just hit yourself with a goddamn hammer!" Beth wanted to scream but realized that it would be far from prudent to yell at a man with a hammer, much less one willing to use it on himself, and least of all one she was entirely reliant on for the foreseeable future. She chose careful, neutral words.

"You're bruising."

"I hit myself with a hammer."

Beth decided on a different tack. "Okay, *why* did you hit yourself with a hammer?" She spoke as if to a child, hoping to suppress any hint of panic but realizing she felt none.

"To illustrate," he explained. "There are things down here that can hurt us."

"I did not doubt that."

"You sounded unsure. It is best to be sure about such things."

"Are there things that can harm us if we do not choose to harm ourselves?"

Rake thought for a moment. "Something could fall on us."

Beth realized she had not seen a single thing fall. That was odd. Despite the many precariously stacked shelves and crumbling bricks and dingy cellars, nothing had fallen. Not even a speck of dust.

Come to think of it, she hadn't seen any dust at all. Why was there no dust? She breathed in deeply. No allergies, no asthma. Ordinarily, the briefest stint in a place like this would have sent her into a fit of coughing, wheezing, and sniffling. Something didn't add up.

"Why is the air clean?" she asked.

"What else would air be?"

"Dusty?"

"Would you prefer it that way?"

Beth shook her head. "What I prefer has nothing to do with it."

"Maybe." He looked at her. "Why are you complaining if you have what you want?"

"I'm not complain—" she began, but broke off in a pout. "Look, there's no dust, nothing falling, nothing dangerous. At least, nothing we've seen. But you still haven't told me whether we're actually safe here." She quickly amended. "Safe from things that can harm us."

The pause which followed worried Beth more than dust or falling objects or rats. Up until now, there had been no uncertainty from Rake. Not when it came to things which mattered. His memory seemed a little fuzzy in places, but only concerning his own past. He seemed to know everything about this place. Or at least he acted like he did. Now he seemed uncertain.

But uncertain about what? Beth hoped it

wasn't about her. Had she crossed a line without knowing it? Maybe she had come across as too suspicious and this made her a problem. Rake had been kind to her, and she did not want to be a problem. It probably wouldn't be a mere matter of degree either. He would view the dichotomy as absolute and unambiguous, much as he did the distinction between above and below. She was either his traveling companion *or* a problem, and the transition would be sudden. She liked the way he treated her as a companion and had no desire to learn how he would behave toward a problem.

"I was wrong to ask you to clarify," Rake replied at length.

The words startled Beth from her reverie. "Clarify what?"

"About safety."

"Ah, so you finally admit it!" Beth grinned and put her hands on her hips. "The guru-talk is an act. It's hard to keep it up, eh?"

Now it was Rake's turn to look confused. "Guru-talk?"

"The stuff you say."

"I say what I say. You say what you say. Why would what I say be one thing and what you say be another?"

"Exactly. Stuff like that."

"I see. It is in your nature to name things. There is no harm in this. I will name your speech in return."

A minute passed, and Beth began to suspect he had lost his train of thought. "Well?" she prompted. "What do you name it?"

"I did not say I would do so right away. A name

is not something to be given lightly, and nothing immediately comes to mind."

Beth smiled. "Well, that's a first."

"Does this upset you?"

Beth laughed. "Not at all. You were about to explain why you were wrong and I was right."

She had assumed he would require a moment to recall what he was saying, but he spoke as if there had been no interruption. Had he patiently been biding his time through her antics? Humoring her? This raised a fresh concern. Even if he did not turn on her, he could end up viewing her as a child. Part of her suspected he already did, and perhaps had all along. This did not bother her as much as the fact she was okay with it. Such a thing would be demeaning, but also comforting in its own way.

"You did not need to clarify what it meant to be safe," Rake elaborated. "That does not matter."

"Safety seems like it should matter." Beth wasn't sure whether she just wanted to be argumentative now that he was agreeing with her.

"*Seems* and *is* are different."

Beth gave a smirk, but it was a warm smirk and her eyes lingered on Rake.

"All right, why doesn't it matter what I meant?" she asked when nothing more was forthcoming.

"We are safe from everything here. Therefore, there is no need to enumerate specific concerns."

She was about to point out that he *had* hurt himself, but she caught herself. The bruise was gone. Had it actually healed quickly or did she simply perceive it that way? If only she knew how much time had passed since the injury. Beth wished she had her watch but was glad she did not.

"Why are you so sure that nothing can harm us?"

"Nothing has."

"That doesn't mean nothing *can*."

Rake smiled. "This is astute of you. I did not say that nothing can harm us. But nothing *will*. I have been walking these paths for a long time. I have developed a good sense of what will or will not happen. That can be more useful that merely knowing what can or cannot happen."

"How long?"

"How long what?"

"You said you have been walking these paths for a long time. How long?"

He shrugged. "I do not remember."

"It seems like something worth remembering."

"Quite the contrary. It is something decidedly not worth remembering. There is value in not remembering such things." Rake sighed. "That is why I do not live above."

"Because you would have to remember such things?" Beth asked. What could have happened that made him prefer to hide in a place like this?

"I do not wish to think that way." He gave her a sympathetic look. "It is the way people above think. They assign great significance to the minutiae of their lives."

Beth had readied a snarky comment about senility, but it now seemed out of place. She hated wasting snarky comments and hoped it would find use later. Another rebuttal presented itself, ready and able.

"Only minutiae like these matter, then." She

waved at a wall filled with a collection of door handles, each beckoning to be chosen.

"The entire world is minutiae when examined closely enough. Imagining *your* minutiae to be of significance is little more than narcissism." There was a slightly sterner quality to his voice.

Beth was tempted to reply with more sarcasm, especially in the face of what was obviously a sore point for him. However, she no longer wanted to see him flustered, at least not that way. But she also did not wish to squander this rare communicativeness of his. Perhaps she finally would get some answers. Real answers.

She wondered why Rake never seemed to grow weary of her questions. Or at least he never let on if he did. This was a novelty to Beth. Up above, she often peppered people with questions. It was a standard tactic, and one which infected her ordinary speech as well. "Up above"? Was she now separating the two like he did? This place was part of the same world, and so was he. Why *wasn't* he bothered by her questions? Everyone else was.

Unfortunately, his tolerance didn't extend to offering useful answers. He always sounded so evasive. At least, that's what her professional self would have called it. Was this his way of punishing her for asking?

It didn't seem like it. Beth didn't doubt his intentions, only his sanity. The absurdity of this struck her, and she began to laugh uncontrollably. The one person in the world she unequivocally chose *not* to doubt was a madman. Maybe that was the way it had to be. It made sense in a perverse way. Only an insane person would not lie.

"Are you all right?" Rake asked as Beth struggled to regain her composure. She managed to stop tittering and took a deep breath. He would have to pony up for seeing her in that state.

"How old are you?" she demanded. "Do you age?"

"We are safe from everything here."

"You said that."

"But you did not hear."

Beth pondered this for a second, her petulance forgotten.

"Everything?"

Rake nodded.

"But not up above?"

"You lived up above. Were you safe there?"

Was that why he left? Beth looked at him, then away. "Rake, you said you're not bound to this place. But can you really return above whenever you wish?"

"One *returns* home. The above is not my home," he replied. Did she catch the slightest touch of soreness in his voice? His face offered no hint.

"I wasn't implying that. I meant can you go there whenever you want?"

"I think so but am not certain. I used to know all the ways in and out, but recently this has changed. That is one reason I don't go above as often. It has become harder to find the entrances."

"What about the exits?" It would not bode well for her if he forgot those.

"There always are exits. They are easier to find."

"Aren't the exits and entrances the same?"

Rake shook his head. "They may start that way, but nothing remains so simple."

"Have you forgotten where the entrances are?"

"Some. Or maybe they have moved."

"But they exist?"

He shrugged. "If an entrance cannot be found, is it an entrance?"

"What if it can be found by some but not others?"

"That is indeed a possibility, but not a relevant one. If an entrance can be found, I can find it. Or at least it has been that way thus far."

Beth raised her finger and did her best imitation of him. "You mean 'will be found'. 'Will be' is more important than 'can be'."

Rake gave a chuckle, and Beth's jaw dropped. It was the first time she had seen him do such a thing. His face was dazzling.

"I suppose you are learning, after all," he replied. "If an entrance will be found, then I will find it."

Beth ordinarily would have bristled if anyone addressed her in such a condescending manner, but from him it felt natural. Besides, she hadn't yet recovered from her shock.

After a few seconds, she smiled. "That makes it easy, then. Once we're up above, all I need to do is find an entrance you didn't notice. Then I'll have proven you wrong."

"And what will that achieve?"

"If you can be wrong about that, then you can be wrong about everything." She casually continued her imitation of him before realizing he was staring at her. Suddenly, she felt very shy.

"You have assumed that I cannot be wrong about

anything? I am flattered, but this is rather foolish of you."

Beth *did* bristle at that.

"All the more reason to show you up," she snapped back, eager to pass off her annoyance as playfulness.

Rake raised an eyebrow. "You would prefer that I be wrong? It seems odd to wish this of the man guiding you through the countless paths down here."

Put that way, it did sound pretty idiotic. What exactly was she playing at? Beth wondered whether she had left her common sense up above. Her focus was acutely drawn to the word "man". Of all the things he had said, why did *this* catch her ear? She realized it was the first time he had applied that word to himself. It implied he was alive, or at least that he viewed himself that way. She was not sure whether this was a good or bad thing.

Part of her had hoped that her inexplicable docility was the result of some sort of spell. If he was just a man, she would have to brook more ... troublesome explanations. It would mean she had been following some random guy around like an obedient little puppy, an intolerable thought at best. Most worrisome of all, he no longer would be an inaccessible abstraction. They would be equals, and this would reframe everything that had happened. Her feelings for him could be given form. They would have implications, and she would have to decide whether to act on them. It would complicate everything.

"You are mistaken about one thing, though," Rake continued.

Beth looked up, grateful for the distraction from

her growing unease and praying his next words wouldn't magnify it.

"I would not be wrong," he explained. "If you find an entrance, I will find it through you. The outcome is the same. Assigning causation is pointless. Who is to say that you are not my means of finding the entrance? Or that I would not have found it some other way without you?"

Beth had no desire to indulge an increasingly academic philosophical discussion. "Okay, let's assume you can ... will find these exits. *How* do you find them?"

"I just do."

This sounded less like arrogance than unflappable confidence. Beth decided somebody had to flap it. Better to have a less confident guide who didn't get lost than an overconfident one who did.

"But don't you ever get lost?" Beth insisted.

"Not here. Only above."

"I don't see how. There are no signs down here, and no..." She was about to say "light" but looked around. "Well, there's light but it has no source I can find."

Rake shrugged. "Just because you cannot find something does not mean it is not there. The same is true of exits. Correspondingly, just because something is there does not mean you can find it. Though, perhaps *you* will."

Beth tried to refute his circuitous reasoning but failed to find the desired contradiction. She wondered whether she was misinterpreting his words. It was a growing feeling she had about everything he said. Maybe he was trying to lead her to a certain understanding but she insisted on straying instead. If so, it would be entirely his fault. If he wanted her to have a certain understanding, he simply should provide it.

"You need not worry about the light," Rake continued. "You cannot see its source because light does not illuminate itself. To see the source requires a source."

"But light comes *from* the source. It's where the light is strongest."

"Is there a source for the breeze on your face or the background noise you hear?"

"There is no breeze or background noise down here," Beth pointed out.

Rake's eyes did not waver. "From myriad small things may emerge a perception we cannot impute to any specific one of them. Above, the sources of light are simple and obvious. Here, they are not."

"You're saying everything down here glows?" Beth wondered if that meant she was glowing too.

Rake shook his head. "I am saying you should not assume that your understanding is applicable."

"Then you tell me: where *does* the light come from?"

"That is something we each must discover for ourselves."

Beth spent the next few minutes fuming before deciding it would accomplish nothing. As little as she gleaned from Rake's answers, she gleaned less from his silence. Frustrated or not, she would have to ask more questions. It was what she did for a living, so why was it so difficult here? She realized the fundamental difference. There was no judge who could coerce answers. Was this what the world was like without a referee to play to? She was forced to directly contend with another's will. She had no leverage over the man, and there was nobody she could manipulate into offering leverage.

"Does it come from us?" she asked, unsure what else to start with. It was a possibility, if an implausible one. On the other hand, the alternatives were equally implausible.

Rake smiled. "That is not entirely wrong."

"How generous," Beth griped. "I'm glad you don't consider me a complete fool."

Rake gave her a slightly puzzled looked before continuing. "Light would serve no purpose without someone to see it. If it existed, its existence would go unremarked. The same could be said of this entire place."

Before Beth could ask anything else, he stopped and turned toward her. "It seems that something has come to preoccupy you."

She suddenly felt ashamed. He was the one with poor communication skills? She had been poking and prodding without saying what really bothered her.

She took a deep breath. "Well, I am being led through an inexplicable subterranean world by a complete stranger who claims he never gets lost. Oh, and I don't need to eat or sleep and there's a magical light everywhere we go."

Rake smiled. "This bothers you?"

"Wouldn't it bother you?"

Rake shook his head. "I do not think so. If it bothered me, I would not do it."

"What if you started, only to realize how foolish it was later?"

"Is that how you feel?"

Beth stopped herself. Was she about to inadvertently and decisively reject the man?

"No, I don't. And that is a problem too."

"Why? I do not feel that way either, and it is not a problem."

"Our roles are not symmetric. You could find your way out at will, and nobody has cast a spell on you, making you oblivious to danger."

"A spell?"

Beth stepped back and stared at him. "How else can you explain it?"

"It is strange that you require a spell to do what you want." Rake looked at her closely. "Is it always this way up above?"

Beth groaned. "That's not what I mean."

"There is no magic here, unless you brought it with you."

"Just forget I said anything." She didn't exactly regret opening up to him about this particular concern, and she certainly hadn't expected him to understand, but his dismissiveness disappointed her anyway. Wasn't a man supposed to be supportive?

She cleared her throat. "However, that doesn't address the more important question. You said you can find the way out, but why should I believe you?"

"It would have been best not to accept my help if you were not prepared to believe me."

Beth gave Rake a sharp look, and he continued. "But it seems that is not what you meant. You worry I will get lost."

"Exactly."

"Or that I will abandon you."

Beth stopped. She had indeed considered the possibility, but not recently. Hearing it articulated by Rake was something else entirely. Was it a threat?

"Neither need concern you," he assured her.

Beth pursed her lips. "Believe it or not, being told not to worry by the guy who is the source of my worry won't stop me from worrying. *Why* needn't it concern me?"

"You do not need me to find the way out."

"In what world do you imagine I could find my way out?" She gestured at the room.

"This world. You need only step through a door and you are out of this space."

"You know what I mean," Beth snapped, struggling to control her voice. Apparently, whatever spell quieted her fear did not do the same for her temper.

Rake did not seem to notice. "You are underestimating yourself. That can happen down here. As I once said, this place can be disorienting."

Beth had no recollection of such a warning but decided to stay on the topic at hand. "That's the whole point. It's disorienting, so I can't find my way out. That's what happens when someone's disoriented."

Rake shook his head. "One does not follow from the other. Have you gotten lost here?"

"You've been leading me."

"If I stop now, do you know the way?"

Beth almost panicked but did not. She put her hand on his arm and smiled. "Please don't."

Her words had been intended as a rebuke but

came out soft, almost sultry. Something about touching him electrified her. Was she excited to be at his mercy? She didn't feel like she was at his mercy. If anything, the entire exchange had the flavor of teasing between friends. But the truth remained that she *didn't* know him. He could take away a very different impression of their conversation. It wouldn't be the first time such a thing had happened to her.

"I won't unless you wish me to," he promised. "However, you could find the way. You would be surprised how easy it is."

Beth very much doubted this. She had paid scant attention to their route and only vaguely registered her surroundings most of the time. This was part of the reason she never hiked alone. She had learned through hard experience that she always would lose the trail.

As if to illustrate this incontrovertible truth, Beth looked around and was astonished. How had she not noticed *this*? They were standing in the middle of what looked like a mall. There were no signs, so it was hard to be sure. The interior seemed oddly compressed, and she couldn't quite make out what was in the stores. The windows were dirty or maybe dark. Something resembling bloated manikins appeared behind one of them. Beth stared in wonder, willing her head to turn but unable to make it do so. She prayed she would succeed in averting her eyes before something happened. Just as she managed to, she caught a glimpse of movement at the periphery of her vision. She hoped it wasn't one of the manikins but somehow knew it was.

Beth closed her eyes and made an effort to calm herself before realizing there was no need. She remembered her original purpose: to test Rake's theory. She tried to imagine the correct way forward. Why hadn't she closed her eyes in the first place? That would have been easier than forcing her head to turn, and she would have been able to pretend a little longer.

She focused on her task, praying that nothing would emerge from the stores while she was helpless. Or worse, perhaps she would open her eyes to find herself in one. Would the way forward appear like magic? Maybe there would be a big neon arrow. She almost laughed.

Of course there was nothing. This mystic mumbo jumbo never worked. If you closed your eyes, the universe didn't talk to you. You just stumbled around in the dark. Maybe it would be good practice for when the lights went out. No, Rake had promised. Yes, he *had* promised. But there was something else, something that continued to bother her.

"If it's so easy, how did the others get lost?" Beth asked, opening her eyes with a newfound confidence that Rake was wrong. "You said many have."

"I did not say that *they* could find the way."

"Why am I different?"

"I invited you and you accepted the invitation."

Beth didn't buy it. Something told her that she wasn't his first companion down here, but she decided not to inquire too closely at the moment. Ferreting out such a truth could be disadvantageous if it was the wrong truth.

"I'm still dependent on you, though," she replied. "Under your protection, so to speak." Something about the prospect thrilled her. "I'm sorry I've turned out to be less able than you hoped."

Rake shook his head. "You misunderstand. The invitation and its acceptance were symptoms not causes. The type of person who would be invited and who would accept the invitation is the type of person who will be able to navigate the below. The type of person *it* will accept."

"But you said to 'stay close' when we started. Obviously, it can't be intrinsic to me."

The smallest hint of a smile graced Rake's mouth. He obviously was pleased she had recollected his words.

"A person who *can* succeed at something does not simply do so," he explained. "They must acquire proficiency. But a person who cannot succeed at something never will. They would not receive the invitation or be inclined to accept it if proffered."

"Then how would they wind up down here?"

"There are many ways. They could find an entrance or an entrance could find them. Or they could follow me in without an invitation. That has happened before." He gave her a pointed look, and Beth remembered that she and her sister had done exactly this.

She stifled a shudder. "What do you do to them?"

"If I discover them, I try to help. Sometimes they do not wish for help. They may be inclined to run or fight or hide. I do my best, but I can do no more."

Judging by Rake's patience with her, Beth imagined an intruder would have to be terribly troublesome or unlucky to fail to avail themselves of Rake's help.

"Barring that, you guide them out?"

"I try to help them. If they wish to return above, I guide them there."

"Doesn't everyone want to?" Beth asked. She had a hard time envisioning someone who would not, other than Rake.

"Do you?"

With a start, Beth realized that she did not. The whole time they had been down here, it wasn't only that she felt no fear. She felt no connection to the world above. Was that because she was certain she would return there soon? Maybe this all was some sort of holiday to her.

"I'm down here for a purpose," she declared. "I'm confident you'll lead me out when we've reached the end of our trip, so I'm in no rush."

Rake said nothing, and she wished he would at least offer some affirmation.

"Do you know what becomes of them?" Beth asked at length. She had been afraid to do so earlier but no longer felt any such compunction. After all, he had empowered her. Even if he one day chose to abandon her, she would be able to find her own way out. If she believed him. But if she didn't believe him about this there was no reason to believe him about anything, and that was a road she would rather not travel. Nonetheless, she hoped he would not abandon her and knew he would not.

"Nobody truly knows what becomes of anyone else," Rake replied.

Beth gave him a hard look, and he shrugged. "I do not know. Perhaps they wander down here like me. Or perhaps they have perished. I like to think they are content with whatever path they have found."

It was hard for Beth to imagine that anyone would be content groping in the unceasing darkness of this vast deep. Just because she felt no fear didn't mean *they* wouldn't. And she had light — or at least Rake did. She would have to ask him about that. Was she special enough to merit light of her own? Beth suspected that her tranquility would only last as long as the light. What did those other people become down here? What did they do to survive? Maybe they became Rake.

"Is that how you ended up here?" she asked. "Did you wander in one day?"

"I do not remember."

Beth was about to comment on how conveniently porous his memory was but thought better of it. Maybe he really *didn't* remember, though it probably was merely his way of avoiding inconvenient questions. She decided it didn't matter. She would keep asking questions, and eventually he would slip up. In her experience, they always did. Of course, she never had encountered anyone like him. But he *had* lived above, so he was like everyone else in some sense.

Lived.

This was the word he used. She had assumed he meant in contrast to living down here now, but there was another way to read it as well.

People lost in the endless deep dark. There was a

name she could think of for such a place.

―•―

During the next few hours or days, Beth mulled over how to broach the subject. She doubted that Rake would grow impatient with retreading familiar territory, but to make any headway she would have to frame things correctly.

If she asked about him, she would get another cryptic answer — and if she asked about the place, he may not know. It was possible that he just performed a role, with no idea for whom or what purpose. The best avenue was to make it about *her*.

Unlike most people Beth knew, she was quite bad at centering the world on herself. Her profession frowned upon doing so, and she never had developed the instinct elsewhere. Ultimately, she settled on an approach so simple that she was embarrassed how much deliberation it had required.

"You said this isn't a dream," Beth noted, apropos of nothing.

"If it is, it is a very long one. I do not think we will awaken from it."

We. Putting aside how pleased she was that he coupled their destinies like this, it also could be construed as a hint at the fate this place had in store for her. Perhaps she too would end up ferrying lost souls, answering barrages of questions with abstruse adages.

"Am I dead?" she asked, unable to think of a tidy segue.

"No."

Beth was stunned. It was as direct a response as she could have hoped for. Well, if he was in a giving mood maybe she should test some other possibilities.

"Then, we're in a different plane?"

Rake raised an eyebrow. "I'm not sure what you mean. We're below, and the world you know is above."

"But don't they exist in different times or places somehow?"

Rake seemed equally confused by this question.

"Can you get to one from the other?" Beth clarified.

"You came here, and I went there. What else do you mean?"

She felt embarrassed. "I don't know. You read about this sort of thing in books."

"Read different books."

"That's rather patronizing," Beth fumed.

"Am I wrong?"

Beth decided not to lose her cool. She wanted answers, and browbeating him would not win her any.

"What will happen when I return?" she asked, her voice a touch sharper than she preferred. "Will it be a hundred years later?"

"Do you think our trip will take a hundred years?"

"Maybe time passes differently here."

"Then it wouldn't be time. The passage of what we call time does not change when you enter a cave. Why would it be different here?"

"This isn't a cave," Beth objected. "Would you

know if time differed down here? You don't use a clock."

Rake looked at her. "You seem to have confused yourself." He gently touched her forehead with his finger, making her heart flutter. "That is nothing to be ashamed of. This place can be disorienting if you are not used to it. If you went above right now, it would be a little over a week since you left. Time is the same here. This is not a different world, and you are not dead in it."

"Then why don't I need food or water?"

"As I said, we are safe from everything here."

"Everything?"

Rake gave a wry smile. "Not doubt."

"Is that because I'm with you, or is it true for everyone?"

"Doubt is universal, understanding is not."

Beth grimaced as she suppressed the urge to take issue with yet another vapid maxim. She took a deep breath and collected herself.

"Is safety universal too?" she asked. Perhaps it was a matter of couching things in his language.

"I do not know. I have not met everyone."

There was no snippiness in his words, and Beth decided it was not intended as a rebuke, just more of his pedantry.

"I think I see," she announced after a few moments.

"Do you?"

"This place is part of the world above."

Rake graced her with an indulgent smile. "Indeed. It could be nothing else."

"But what *is* this, then? It's not a cave, and I'm

pretty sure none of the things we see were brought here."

"It is as I said earlier. This place is a shadow of the above." Rake gestured at the space they were in, some sort of large, messy office. "These are the echos of human habitations, and the paths are the holes between."

A distant creak caught Beth's attention. It was not the first she had heard, but it was the loudest. What troubled her was not only that the sounds trailed her, but that they seemed to be getting closer. Rake must have noticed this as well, and she was somewhat comforted by his lack of concern. Or maybe he *didn't* hear them. If he truly was safe from all harm, would he have any need to notice such things? He had claimed she was safe as well, but right now Beth didn't feel very safe at all. She instinctively clutched Rake's arm. He looked down at her with big inscrutable eyes.

"Do those echoes include people?" she asked, her eyes on the dim light of the path behind them.

Rake smiled. "If they did, you would be surrounded by them."

Beth abruptly pulled away, annoyed at herself for asking such a silly question and at him for pointing it out. Then she realized it *wasn't* a silly question.

"That doesn't follow," she objected. "Clearly, not *everything* is replicated down here."

"Nothing is 'replicated'," Rake corrected. "These are echoes, not copies."

Beth wanted to ask what the difference was but didn't wish to lose her thread.

"Okay, but these 'echoes' aren't of *everything*.

Otherwise, this place would be an impenetrable clutter. Clearly, only some things have echoes."

"That may be correct."

"You don't know?" Once again, she couldn't tell whether Rake was genuinely unsure or being evasive. It was hard to imagine a reason for him to be. Or at least a reason which wouldn't cascade into a long list of other reasons that implied nothing good.

"I have no way of knowing," he explained. "I have not explored the entirety of the below, and I do not know the entirety of the above. How can I compare them?"

"A simple calculation would suffice," Beth proposed.

Rake shook his head. "Maybe several things have the same echo or one thing has several echoes. It also is possible that the echoes do not resemble the originals in any obvious way." He gestured at a burlap sack in a corner of the tunnel they had emerged into. "That could be the echo of a house or a pen. There is no way to be certain."

"Why would they look different?"

"Why would they look the same? We do not know why there are echoes, so we cannot know how they take these forms or what they are echoes of."

Beth looked at him. "Well, that supports my point. If people have echoes too, it does not follow that *everyone* would have an echo down here. Maybe only a few do."

"Or their echoes could be things."

Beth would *not* let this turn into one of his abstract discursions.

"Anyway, I'm just saying that there could be people down here who are echoes of people above."

"Or of things above," Rake observed.

"Fine. But my point holds. How do you know there aren't?"

"I have never met any."

"But there *are* others here. You said so."

Rake shook his head. "They are not echoes. I told you they found a way in."

There was no exasperation in his voice, even though she felt like she was covering the same ground over and over. Beth wondered what it would take to make the man grow impatient. She always felt on the verge of it, yet somehow never managed to. On the other hand, he *always* managed to make her feel impatient. It was asymmetric warfare.

"Or you invite them in," Beth suggested.

She wondered whether she sounded suspicious of him. It was not her intention to, but she couldn't shake old habits. Besides, some concern was warranted. There could be a marked difference between the type of individual invited by him and one who randomly stumbled on the place — or worse yet, followed him in uninvited. She wanted to know what sort of people she was likely to encounter. On the other hand, they hadn't encountered *anyone* up until now. Maybe meeting someone was exceptionally unlikely.

In that case, the noises could be innocuous. This place ordinarily was silent and still. She and Rake were the only obvious disturbances. Perhaps their own passage was the culprit. If the things here were unaccustomed to visitors, the slightest air movement or vibration could upset their precarious balance. Maybe the sounds she was hearing were aftereffects. Things toppling or settling into their new places once the silence and stillness returned. That would explain why the creaking seemed to follow her.

"I brought *you* here," Rake pointed out, interrupting her ruminations.

Beth liked to feel special, but she wondered how special she really was.

"Any others?" she asked.

Rake didn't flinch, and she wondered why she had expected him to. It wasn't as if he had cheated on her — especially since these would be in his past — but there could be unpleasant stories behind them. Was she merely the latest in a long line of failures?

He thought for a few moments before replying. "Yes."

Beth groaned, less from disappointment at not being unique than frustration at his uninformative response. Back to pulling teeth.

"How many," she demanded.

"I don't recall. It has been a long time."

"What happened to them?" Her eyes were fixed on him.

"I don't recall that either."

Once again his poor memory came to the rescue, and once again something convinced Beth that he was being truthful. This was some small comfort, though she wasn't sure why. If anything, it should have worried her more. Tragic-but-mourned would be bad enough, but completely-forgotten? What exactly did that make *her* to him? Maybe she wouldn't even be a statistic.

Another worry slowly materialized. What if they ran into one of those past failures? She had assumed they perished miserably, but perhaps they had not. Come to think of it, why did she assume they were 'failures' or had perished at all? Maybe Rake led them to their promised destinations. Maybe they were home and happy above, and their fates simply weren't noteworthy enough to merit remembrance.

Why, then, were there no stories of this place? Did those he rescued forget their time with him? Perhaps they remained silent out of gratitude to Rake. Both seemed improbable.

If some of those others were down here she *could* run into one, and that could end badly for many reasons. They could hate Rake for having abandoned them or betrayed them or whatever he did which he so conveniently forgot. Or they could resent *her*, their replacement and the perfection of what he had failed to achieve with them. Wouldn't *she* feel that way seeing a new woman on his arm?

Beth wondered why she was so certain they all were women. Maybe he had invited men too. She was tempted to ask but was sure he would claim he didn't recall. Perhaps he *did* remember but was protecting their privacy. Beth certainly wouldn't want the world to know about her own ridiculous escapade. At the very least, it reflected poorly on her judgment. And what did it say that she actually *wanted* Rake? He certainly wasn't the sort of guy she could take to a party or introduce to her mother.

Beth froze. Her general worries aside, *that* could be a real problem. Presumably, Rake was guiding her to her mother. What if he insisted on meeting her? How could she deny the man who had made the visit possible, who had done so much for her, whom she keenly did not wish to deny? Beth would have to find some way to deal with this. For the first time, she felt truly anxious.

"Are you all right?"

Rake was standing over her, and Beth realized she was doubled over and staring at the ground. Looking up, she saw concern in his eyes. And doubt. Doubt about her, or doubt that he could help her? Was that what it was like to watch a pet suffer? Despite herself, something about the thought warmed Beth.

She smiled up at him before slowly straightening.

"Were you worried about me?"

His expression did not change. "I was worried for you."

"I thought you said we are safe down here," Beth laughed. Let him chew on *that*. She suddenly felt petty for turning his concern against him. She also wasn't sure why she wanted him to acknowledge that they *weren't* safe.

Before he could reply, she quietly hugged him and whispered, "thank you."

With a start, Beth realized what she was doing and stepped back. She prayed she didn't look as embarrassed as she felt. She had to do something to defuse the awkwardness. A question in the right direction, *any* direction. Then she remembered that there *was* something which troubled her, something legitimate. However much she tried to dismiss it as such, she knew the rustling wasn't just objects settling.

"Are the others good or bad?" she asked, composing herself as best she could. Her voice was stilted.

"I don't recall them," Rake replied, and Beth realized he thought she was still talking about the ones he had invited. The man's forbearance once again struck her as nothing short of saintly. She wouldn't have had one thousandth of his patience.

She shook her head. "I mean the people who are here without your consent. Are they good or bad?" Mere curiosity wasn't a crime, but the type of person who would secretly trail a stranger into a cave likely didn't have anything honorable in mind.

"Such words have no meaning."

Beth kicked herself for not anticipating this answer. If beauty has no meaning, neither would every other subjective classification. She stopped herself. Was she enjoying this? It was yet another pointless academic digression.

Beth suddenly realized why she felt so comfortable conversing with Rake — and why his answers failed to infuriate her, despite frustrating her to no end. It was like school. This was the sort of semantic nitpicking they would play at in class. It almost felt nostalgic. All that was missing were frequent cries of "Objection!"

Such academic debate had little place in the real world, and she no longer was in fine fettle. However, this epiphany gave Beth the tool she needed. Why hadn't she realized it sooner? She was no stranger to this sort of debate and just needed to dust off long-neglected skills. Beth considered how to properly reformulate her question, but Rake elaborated before she had the opportunity.

"They are like anyone else. Some are what you would call good, some are what you would call bad. Other people may call them something else."

"Call them what?"

"I do not know what other people call things."

"What do *you* call them?"

"Others. They are others." He gestured at the walls. "Like these things. They are not me, so they are others."

"But you said the others are people, not things. These things around you are static. They will be here, unchanged when you return."

"Is that what you think?"

Beth had not considered this. She wouldn't be able to find the way back if there *was* no way back. Did the paths change? What about the things in them? There was no way to know, or maybe there was no way for *her* to know. He probably knew.

Once again, Beth did not ask because she did not wish to know. She preferred the comfort of imagining that in this deep quiet place, things always would be as they were. That nothing was lost and nothing forgotten. That there remained some place in all the world where such a thing was true.

But the others concerned her. *They* could change things or destroy them. They could remove or remodel or ruin. Perhaps that was what Rake had meant.

"Do the others change them?" she asked.

"I am sure they can. I do not know if they do."

Beth was about to demand clarification, but he looked at her. "You seem needlessly worried. As I said, you are safe. The others cannot harm you. We are safe from everything here."

"But all this? Is *it* safe from them?"

Rake smiled, as if remembering an old joke. "Does that concern you?"

"Don't we need landmarks to navigate by? If things are moved, we could get lost."

"There is no such thing as a landmark."

"But how can you retrace your path?" There was a note of panic in Beth's voice, and she realized she had wrapped herself around Rake's arm again.

"The path each of us treads has only one direction. We cannot retrace anything."

Beth looked up at Rake. She had clung to him longer than ever before and more tightly. He didn't seem to mind her soft pressure on his arm. In anyone else, she would have taken that as a promising sign.

"Then how *do* you navigate?" she asked. He had said she could do so too, but she still had no idea how. Would she suddenly understand how if they were separated? It would be better to learn now, before such a thing happened.

"It is not hard," he explained. "You take a step. A step is always forward, even if you think it is not."

"Is that a property of this place?"

"It is a property of every place."

Beth smirked. "So we are *not* safe from time?"

She couldn't wait to see him try to wriggle out of *that*. This was the problem with guru-talk. Anything could be made to sound profound, but only so much rubbish could be spewed without creating inconsistencies. She loved opponents who exhibited this particular vanity.

Rake shook his head. "You misunderstand. Time does not stop. It cannot. Such a thing has no meaning. Time is the metronome of change, nothing more and nothing less. Change is the source of existence, of thought, and of action. Without it, we cannot speak of time. Time is the measure of change, and change is the measure of existence. We are safe from change, but not from time."

"By your reasoning, that would mean we do not exist."

"It is not *my* reasoning. Reasoning does not belong to me or to you. There is reasoning and there is confusion. It is impossible for existence to prove that it exists, only that it does not."

Beth stared at him. "What does that even *mean*?" She wasn't being combative. She had followed only about half of what he said and was sure it contained more than one critical contradiction, but she was unable to identify any.

"A logic cannot determine its own consistency, only its own inconsistency," Rake explained.

Did he think using a different word made things clearer? Perhaps he was trying to veil the speciousness of his argument. Beth gave a sigh. Why was she taking him seriously?

"A man cannot determine his own consistency, but a woman can determine his inconsistency," she quipped.

Rake said nothing, and she wondered whether he had heard her. Maybe he was offended, though she doubted it in light of how even-tempered he had been so far.

Was this whole thing his way of saying she was too dumb to understand or that he had no real explanation because *he* did not understand. Perhaps understanding could not know that it understood, only that it did not. She wanted to make some such comment, but could not find the right phrasing. Without that it would fall flat, like her previous attempt at a joke. She decided to change gear.

"But the others are not?" Beth asked.

Rake seemed to have been thinking about something else, and his voice had an absent-minded quality. "Not what?"

"Safe from time," she began but quickly corrected to "safe from change."

"Maybe."

Beth stopped in her tracks, but Rake did not.

"Why are we different?" she asked. He had invited *some* of those others in. Why weren't they safe too? Did they do something wrong? Beth felt a shiver down her spine. She had taken for granted that she was special. Chosen. She felt comfortable around Rake, but would he abandon her? He had promised not to, but there could be worse things than abandonment.

"What happens to them?" she asked, her voice slightly chilly. Would he conveniently fail to remember this too?

"I do not know what happens if they stay. Perhaps they change, Perhaps they find ways to survive. As I said, I help those I can."

She sensed he was talking about the others who

strayed in. Maybe the ones he invited got special treatment.

"So once they refuse your aid, you are done with them?"

"Once they refuse my aid, they are done with me. I have nothing else to offer them."

"What if they ask for it later?" Beth had read old tales where the consequences of spurning protection could be grotesque. Such a gift was not to be refused lightly. Maybe he held a grudge when it was.

"That has never happened."

"Because you never meet them, or because you never repeat the offer?"

"The offer remains, though the opportunity may not. If I meet them again, they are free to take me up on it."

This came as a great relief to Beth. He didn't nurse resentment over such a thing. If she were somehow to commit such a folly, she need only find him again and he would guide her. But what if he already was guiding someone else? Would Beth be the creaking sound desperately following in their wake?

"How often do you run into others?" she asked.

"As often as I do. Without a means of demarcating time, there can be no meaning to naming it."

Beth clenched her fists and took a deep breath. Nostalgic or not, his fastidious literalism did wear on her at times. She only could handle so much guru-talk. In hindsight, it struck her as incredibly pompous, though his actual speech never felt that way in the moment. If anything, it felt natural, almost soothing. It also could be downright exasperating. She was beginning to learn how to elicit information but evidently had not mastered the technique. It was like conducting a trial in a foreign country. The general principles were the same, but she did not know the specific rules.

"Have you ever met the same one twice?" she asked after some indeterminate time.

Rake thought for far longer than usual. "I do not believe I have."

So the question of someone changing their mind never came up. But what about the ones he *had* helped? Not seeing them again could be a good sign or a terrible sign. Did he set them on the path to home and safety, or did they meet less enviable fates? Even if it wasn't through malice or neglect, he simply could fail to comprehend their limitations. What was safe for him may not be safe for others.

Or maybe he saw them off and assumed the best, blind to the harsh truths of this world. Could one such as he know those things? She wondered if this would be her fate too. Where exactly *was* he leading her? What he thought she wanted and what she did want could be two very different things. Or did he not care? She wasn't sure which would be better. Why wasn't he like everybody else? Maybe he only was this way to her. He had said this was not how he appeared to everyone. Perhaps he referred to more than just looks.

"How do the others see you?" Beth suddenly asked.

"I do not know. I never have asked them."

"But they aren't afraid of you?"

"I do not know. Maybe I am not the worst thing

they have seen. I could seem normal to them. You see me as beautiful, or what I once thought of as beautiful. Others, perhaps, do not."

Beth couldn't take it anymore and decided to ask him outright.

"What are you?"

"I am a man showing a woman the world he knows. Maybe you will do the same for another one day."

Up to this point, Beth's misgivings — however sensible — had been fleeting. Now she felt real fear. He showed others the way and then never saw them again. He never bothered to learn what had happened to them. Heck, he didn't even remember them. What did that augur for her? She realized what she truly was afraid of.

"Then I won't see you again after this?"

"Perhaps. I am not sure. I do know one thing, though. If we meet, it will be down here. It is too difficult to find anything up above, least of all what one wishes to find. Here, it may be different. The paths are many but narrow. It may be possible, at least for us."

These last words thrilled Beth, and her fear dissipated. She felt close, closer than ever before.

"But you said you never met any of the others a second time."

"You are not one of the others."

Beth gave a coquettish pout. "I'll bet you say that to all the girls."

"They would not have asked."

Would not? Why was he speculating? Maybe she *was* the first he truly had invited. If he didn't remember, he could be mistaken that there had been any. This seemed unlikely. The whole process was too familiar to him, like something he had done countless times before. Perhaps there was a reason those others would not have asked such a thing.

Beth really wasn't sure what to make of all this. Was she not one of the others *yet* or was she altogether different? She knew what she wanted the answer to be. She had not known before, or had not accepted it. But she knew now.

She looked up at him, her eyes pleading. "Then what am I? What am I to *you*?"

To her surprise, Rake stopped and seemed unsure of himself. He likely was pondering what to say or how to say it. Or maybe he was staring at a speck of dust on the wall — though there was no dust down here, so probably not that. Dammit, why couldn't the man be more transparent?

Now that they had stopped, Beth examined her surroundings. They were in an odd room, if it could be called a room at all. If there was a ceiling, it was too high to discern. The walls, such as they were, had a peculiar geometry. Colors were more pronounced than in other spaces they had passed through. Was the lighting different or was everything actually more vibrant here?

Scattered around the place were wooden and plastic objects. Beth didn't recognize any and had a hard time fathoming their uses, but it was obvious they were toys of some sort. She couldn't tell whether the place was meant to be an outdoor playground or an indoor playroom. Either way, its purpose was clear.

Something resembling a see-saw was visible in a distant, poorly lit corner. Though she had seen pictures of them, Beth had never encountered one before. Had they gone extinct before she was born? Perhaps she just didn't remember them. How long had it been since she'd set foot in a playground? Maybe if she sat on the see-saw, she would remember. She wondered whether Rake would sit on the other end but suspected he would prove either far too light or far too heavy.

Beth was about to move toward the see-saw when she noticed an ever-so-slight shaking. Straining her eyes, she could make out something large on one end. There was nothing unusual about an object randomly being there. This whole world was filled with random things in random places. The subtle rocking of the elevated end troubled her. *That* was unusual. Nothing moved down here, not unless she or Rake touched it. Was the thing trying to get up? She imagined an obese child wobbling itself off the end.

Beth turned toward Rake. He had a sympathetic expression. Was this his way of reassuring her? That would mean he had seen it too. Maybe he no longer could hide the truth of this place. Would she finally get some real answers?

"I do not know," Rake announced after a few moments. Beth felt her stomach sink. If he didn't know what that thing was, how could he know they were safe from it? Perhaps there was a reason they hadn't come across anything living.

"I'm sorry," he explained. "This is the first time I have done this for someone."

"This?" Beth almost screamed. What the hell did he mean by "this"? Was he about to pull the rug out from under her?

"This," he repeated, gesturing at her and then himself.

Beth realized he was replying to her earlier question. All her worry and hope had been misplaced. Well, not *all*. There did remain the matter of the obese child. Was that her imagination? Maybe Rake had seen it but didn't consider the thing a threat. Either way, it clearly wasn't something she need worry about.

Despite her relief at this, Beth was disappointed with Rake. He at least could have offered a few sweet words. She sighed. Of course he wouldn't. The man probably didn't know how to. Beth considered the words he *had* offered.

"I thought you led others here before," she pointed out.

"Those were different. There was something given, and something taken. That is the way it always has been."

"Something given?"

He looked at her. "And something taken."

Beth shuddered. "What was taken?"

"That is between the giver and the taker. It would be indiscreet to speak of it to another."

Beth was unsure if this was some sort of innuendo or something more sinister. She felt like she had fallen into the pages of a bad novel and really wished she knew whether it belonged in the romance or horror aisle.

"I don't remember giving or taking anything,"

Beth replied. She wondered whether the memory of it was part of the taking. If so, why would he bring it up?

"As I said, you are not like the others."

"But why *me*?" Even if it took her a thousand tries, she would get an answer. It may or may not be the answer she wanted, but she would get his damned answer. She at least would accomplish that much.

"I do not know."

Or not. Her eyes blazed, but he did not seem to notice.

"I simply felt like it," Rake continued. "I was drawn to you."

Beth's body relaxed. There she had it. Her answer. Was it the one she wanted? It did not matter. It was an answer. But her victory was premature. Rake was staring at her. Was he going to kiss her or hit her?

He smiled. "What about you? You strike me as a cautious woman."

She wasn't sure whether this was meant as a compliment. Cautious usually implied unexciting. And how did he know that about her? It wouldn't require any great leap, she supposed. It probably was written all over her face. Her incessant interrogation of him certainly made it clear enough.

"Do you normally follow strange men into dark places?" Rake asked when she said nothing.

Was he about to turn psycho? Horror aisle it was. Beth still felt no fear. Once again, she wondered whether there was some sort of drug at work. Was the air mixed with happy gas? Now that she thought about it, this was quite plausible. All sorts of toxic fumes could be present deep beneath the ground. She wished she had a canary. Actually, any sign of life would be welcome. Even one of Rake's "others". She wondered if the blob on the see-saw qualified.

"Your sister—" he continued.

Was he talking to her? Sister? The word felt alien. Beth realized that she *did* have a sister. This felt like something she ought to remember.

Her mind raced. Was he planning to coax her sister down here too? She wouldn't let him have her! Did he "have" Beth? What was her sister's name? How could she protect her sister if she didn't even know her name?

"—seemed surprised. I gather that such behavior is not typical of you."

Beth looked at her feet. They had not grown tired or blistered this whole time. Another thing she had neglected to notice.

"What are you going to do with me?" she asked.

Something about the question excited her. He could do *anything* to her, as long as it was the sort of anything she wanted.

"The same thing we have been doing. I will lead you."

Beth sighed. The man either was a terrible flirt or a very subtle one. She had a pretty good hunch which and put her hands on her hips.

"That sounds demeaning."

"It is no more demeaning to be led than to lead. If you wish to lead, I will follow."

There was no sarcasm in his words, and once again Beth was unsure whether he was a master of it or entirely unaware of its existence. She shook her head.

"If it suits you better, think of us as walking side by side," Rake offered. "The walls are narrow in places. At times one must lead and one must follow, but it does not matter which."

"Side by side. That is not so bad," she murmured. She took his hand in hers. It wasn't paper-like this time. It was firm, almost impossibly firm, yet far lighter than she would have guessed possible. Was this what came of never eating?

He gave her a quiet smile. "If you wish."

"I wish."

After some time she looked up at him.

"You really have not guided others like me before?"

"It is my first time."

Beth felt her whole body thrill at this. She would have preferred "only time", but "first" would do.

"When you say it is your first time..."

"Walking side by side."

"But you *have* guided others," she persisted. It felt less important, but she still wished to know.

"So I said. Do you doubt that I was truthful about it?" He didn't sound upset, and his grip felt no different.

She shook her head and gave his hand a squeeze. "Indulge me, please."

"I have guided others."

She dropped his hand and fixed him with a cynical stare. "But not like me."

"But not like you."

She wanted this to disarm her suspicion but realized that would be dangerously foolish. He just was repeating what he said before. Was this what he told every woman he lured down here?

"Where are they now?"

"As I said, I do not know. It may have been a long time ago, and I do not remember how many there were."

She took his hand again. "Then you will forget me too."

"Possibly. Does this disappoint you?"

"It does."

"In the world above, everyone forgets."

"Is this place a way of forgetting that world?"

Rake shook his head. "It is the only way of remembering it."

"Up above, there are plenty of ways to remember," Beth absentmindedly observed. This sounded odd to her, and she realized she truly had fallen into his way of referring to "above" and "below" as if they were fundamentally different. For all she knew, "above" was a few meters away. Did it matter? A prisoner could spend her life mere feet from the outside world, yet never know it.

"Nothing is permanent," Rake replied, disrupting her train of thought. "Here or above."

"A lot of this stuff looks like it has been here a long time."

Rake shrugged. "Some things persist longer here, some do not. The difference is that I know my way here. I can find the things I remember, or most of them. Not so above. Once lost, the things above can never be found."

"Isn't that what it means to be lost?" Beth hoped

her lips hadn't curved into a smirk as she said this. It didn't matter; Rake was facing away from her. She wondered why men did this, pontificating to the wall. It was like pacing. For some reason, men always paced when on the phone. She had no explanation for such things but was sure one existed. It probably would illuminate much of what was wrong with men.

"There is a difference between being lost and not being found," Rake pointed out.

"Which is your mother?" Beth asked casually before realizing what she had said. She clasped her hand over her mouth and apologized.

"Why are you apologizing?" Rake asked.

"I shouldn't have said that. I promised to help you find her."

He smiled. "It was a generous sentiment, but unnecessary. I allowed you to make that promise because you needed to."

He *allowed* her to make the promise? This really rankled. Beth managed to calm herself with some effort, albeit less than she would have expected. She would not let herself be distracted, particularly as this was a topic in which she had a keen interest. Nothing offered more insight into a man's character than his relationship with his mother. She had read that in a magazine.

"But what of your mother? Don't you *want* to find her?"

"What is to be gained by finding her? The mother I knew was in the past. If she still exists, she has become something else."

Hadn't he said he was too young to know her

when she left? Perhaps Beth had misunderstood. If so, didn't that mean he *was* incredibly callous after all? No, she knew him better now. He just was dense. She stopped and pointed at him.

"It's not only about *you*. Maybe she wants to see her son. Did you ever consider *her* feelings?" Beth didn't care whether this sounded like an accusation. If an accusation was what it took to get through his thick skull, an accusation it would be.

"Why would she feel differently? We are of the same stock. Our eyes see things the same way."

Something about the words he used bothered Beth. If this place preserved the things above, was his mother one of those things? He seemed to think of her that way, using words like "knew" and "exist". Maybe they would come across her preserved corpse in a rocking chair. Maybe one day Rake would come across *Beth's* preserved corpse. Would he describe her to his latest companion in the same cold, clinical terms?

Beth once again wondered whether his manner of speech was calculated. The use of imprecise words which need not change, however many people or years passed. Were the people in his world as fungible as the things? If she *was* special, perhaps she would merit something more. With equally desiccated words he would describe guiding a specific woman named Beth. He "knew" her, and she "existed". Was it a form of immortality to be memorialized by an unfeeling Charon? It certainly wasn't one she cared for. Beth shook off these thoughts. She had to keep the spotlight on *him*.

"You cannot know that," she insisted. "I can't

believe you assume your mother is the same as you. Don't you care about her at all?" She was astonished how frigid the man could be at times. Did he *know* he was that way? She noticed that Rake was staring at her.

With alarm, Beth realized she may have crossed a line. Not some line drawn in invisible ink by a deluded mind, but one almost anybody would immediately recognize and respect. She tensed. If he hated her, it would be her own damned fault. To have a stranger spit such a thing at you could be deemed unforgivable. Were they strangers? She braced for the storm. Instead, he gently placed his hand on her shoulder. Her body and mind drowned in a rush of sensations, none of which made sense.

"A bond is something which exists when it does," Rake explained. "Once severed, it cannot be recreated." He looked away. "Any more than a person can be restored to life once dead. Another may be born or take their place, but they remain another. The original is gone forever. Seeking to recreate it is pointless."

Was there a message in this about their own bond? Maybe it was a veiled way of telling her to back off. She sensed it would be wise to do so, but her mouth moved of its own accord.

"Then why not create a new bond? She's your mother."

"And I am her son. Yet she has not found me, and I am far easier to find. If she exists, she is something else. Something above. She would not recognize me, nor I her. Even if we met face to face." He gave Beth a pointed look.

"I'm not her," Beth announced, wondering why she felt the need to state something so obvious. Embarrassed, she tried to turn away, but Rake's hand remained on her shoulder. There was no force to it, but it thwarted her anyway. She would have to wriggle free and did not wish to do so. That would break their bond, perhaps forever.

Rake gave a gentle laugh. "I should hope not."

This both pleased and saddened Beth, but she was in the grip of a stronger emotion. She felt tears welling up. Was this how it would be with *her* too? Worse, would she *become* like Rake? She already had trouble remembering her sister's face. On more than one occasion, she even had forgotten she had a sister.

Rake's eyes were sympathetic, as if he knew what she was thinking. "There is no need to grieve over such things. This is the way it is, the way it should be. Without change, we remain the same." His hand returned to his side, freeing her.

"Like your precious tunnels?" Beth snapped, dabbing away her tears.

"They are not my tunnels. They merely are tunnels. I did not make them. Some have been here a very long time."

"That's not what I mean."

"I *know* what you mean. You think too much of this place. You impute strange powers to it. It is not as permanent as you imagine, or as static."

Beth realized he was right. She *had* been building up a mystical image of what was going on. This place certainly was preternatural, but it probably wasn't supernatural. She wasn't dead, and he wasn't some spirit guide. They simply were in a bunch of tunnels, inexplicably paralleling the world she knew. No, not inexplicably. Unexplained. There was a difference. Maybe Rake knew, maybe not. But there *was* an explanation. She just did not have it. Besides, how could she be sure the tunnels actually *did* span the world above?

She and Rake could have been wandering the same small area this whole time. A lot of tunnels could fit in a small space. Would she have noticed if they passed through the same room twice? And if the place wasn't static, they could have traveled the same small loop over and over, experiencing it differently each time.

Did it make any difference? The journey would feel the same. Only the destination would change. Perhaps that was her mistake. Without a destination, the path was all that mattered. But Beth *had* a destination. At least, she felt like she did. Once again, she forced herself back to the conversation.

"What exactly are you?"

"You have asked this before. Do you imagine the answer will change?"

Beth grinned. "Well, maybe *it's* not static either."

Rake shook his head. "You dwell on such a meaningless question."

"You keep evading it."

Rake sighed. "I am me, just as you are you."

"Yet you don't age."

"Neither do you. Not down here."

"So we're immortal." Beth had found her rhythm, firing off retorts and questions with confidence.

"That word has no meaning. I have been here

a long time. I do not know how long I will remain here."

"But you cannot die?"

"I have not so far."

"And you do not age?"

"I have not so far. Not since I have been here."

"How are you sure the same is true of me?"

"Have you aged while you have been here?"

How long *had* she been in this place? Even if time didn't physically pass at a different speed, her perception of it could. Everything here felt distorted, so maybe the passage of time did too. Not so long ago, Rake had mentioned that a week had passed. But when had *that* been? Perhaps years had passed since. Beth pushed aside such thoughts. She decided he was prevaricating as usual.

"I've only been down here a short time," she replied, carefully watching his expression.

"Ah, I see. I forgot how aging works above." He seemed to be pondering the matter. "Yes, I suppose it would take much longer."

Beth cleared her throat. "So, you can't be sure I won't age."

Rake looked at her. "I am sure. I can not say why, but I am."

"That doesn't exactly inspire confidence." But it did.

"How long do you intend to remain down here?" he asked. It was an odd question, especially from someone supposedly leading her to a specific destination. If anyone knew the answer, it should be him. Or did he mean something else?

Beth smiled. "Avoiding wrinkles is every gal's

dream. If it prevents aging, maybe forever."

Rake frowned. "That does not seem like the right reason to remain here. I do not think the place would accept you."

"So I'll be rejected if I try something like that?"

"No, because you will not."

"How can you be sure? Maybe I will."

"It would not have accepted you in the first place if you were the type to do that. Nor would I have invited you."

There was no reproach in his voice, but Beth felt ashamed.

"Do you regret it?" she ventured.

"As I said, I would not have invited you if regret would be the outcome."

"So you do regret it," Beth murmured. Her voice thickened. "An outcome is not something you can see until it happens."

"You misunderstand me, I think. I do not regret it."

They walked in silence for a few minutes.

"What if I lived above, but returned here right before dying?" Beth asked, unable to stop herself.

"You can try. Perhaps others have."

"But it wouldn't work?"

"I do not know."

"If it did, wouldn't you have run into them here?"

"I never have."

"Then maybe it's worth trying."

Rake smiled. "You would not age, but I see no reason that your youth would be restored. Is that what you want?"

"What if I chose to be a young echo of myself?" Beth wasn't sure he would realize she was joking. She wasn't entirely sure she was.

Rake looked confused. "You are not an echo now, so why would you be one then? But you are welcome to try whatever it is that you envision. I did not make the rules of this place, so I do not know them."

For some reason, the conversation had put Beth in a lively mood. Was it the possibility of being ageless? Though she hadn't consciously dwelt on the prospect of death, its inevitability certainly molded her in important ways. Now, she was offered an escape. If she believed that Rake wasn't mad, which probably meant she *was*. In any event, he could be wrong. Maybe he was the only one who didn't age.

"Then why doesn't everybody do this?" Beth asked, bumping into him playfully. "Living here seems a small price to pay to avoid death."

"Is it?" Rake seemed genuinely curious.

Beth nodded. "It certainly strikes me as such."

Rake smiled. "Thwarting death is not the purpose of this place. Death is not meant to be thwarted."

Beth glared at him. "That's easy to say if you're not going to die. The rest of us may have a different opinion."

"I don't remember very well, but there is a reason for death. I used to know such things."

Rake pondered this in silence for a few hours as they walked, and Beth did not wish to disturb him. She had not seen him in such a reverie before and hoped he wouldn't take a wrong turn. However, his body seemed to move of its own accord. She wondered just how many times he had walked these paths.

~•~

At length, Rake stopped. They were in some sort of ruin, or so Beth surmised. A crumbling facade of ornate stucco hosted an array of half-excavated rooms, tops open to the world and populated with furniture in various states of decline. The place looked like the ruins of a stately old mansion but seemed to represent a hodgepodge of different eras. Perhaps it once was a museum?

Something puzzled Beth about the whole scene. There was no weather or rot down here, so why did the furniture look tattered and moldy? If what Rake had said was true, it should be the echo of furniture above. Did that mean the original was this way too? Maybe the process of "echoing" imparted a quality of ruin. Did dragging the essence of a thing into this place damage it? If so, why didn't everything look that way? On the other hand, the building itself was a wreck. Perhaps whatever destroyed it had also damaged its contents.

Beth froze. There was no mistaking it this time. No distant creaking or subtle wobbling or dubious flicker at the periphery of her vision. A shadow had moved. Clearly, distinctly, and directly in front of her. It was in the farthest exposed room of the mansion. She watched for a minute, then two. Nothing. Had it fled down a hole? Maybe the thing was creeping around, quietly flanking her as she stood there like an idiot. Beth desperately wanted to turn but could not force herself to.

She realized she *was* an idiot. Was this how a dog felt staring at its own reflection? The shadow was hers or Rake's. All tension left her body, and she prayed he hadn't seen her childish bout of terror. She turned toward him, but her eyes avoided his, innocently wandering over the walls and ceiling instead.

Then she remembered: there *were* no shadows down here. The light was diffuse. This time, she didn't allow herself to become petrified. She tried to reason it out. Rake did not seem the least bit troubled. If he had seen the thing, he apparently felt no need to comment on it. Beth felt a sudden urgency. She had to warn him of the peril before that thing managed to get behind them, or its friends arrived. Maybe she already was too late.

"I remember now," Rake announced.

Beth looked at him in horror. *Now*? It would have been handy to remember the presence of such things earlier, before they surrounded the two of them and did god knows what. His sangfroid failed to soothe her this time. Were they *with* him? She dismissed the thought. He could have done whatever he wanted with her all along. Unless he was waiting for reinforcements. She remembered the hammer. He didn't need reinforcements.

This had the perverse effect of calming her. If he *was* on her side, the shadow-things posed no threat. Probably. Could a shadow be hurt by a hammer? There wasn't one handy, but there were plenty of other things nearby that Rake could use if need be. Once again, Beth found herself panicking far less than the situation warranted. And once again, she was grateful for this. She returned her attention to Rake.

"Remember what?" she asked, uncertain what such a question invited.

"Why we are not immortal, as you call it, up above."

Beth groaned. He certainly could have picked a better time to emphasize her mortality. And how did he manage to misdirect her? Every. Single. Time.

Was this an attempt to distract her from what was going on? If so, was it meant to comfort her or disarm her? Perhaps he had been cultivating her the whole time, stripping her defenses one by one and readying her for the slaughter. Maybe there was a ritual, and things had to be done in the right order. She had seen something like that in a movie.

Beth reined in her paranoia. She trusted Rake. Not because she wanted to, but because she had to. At this point, there was no other choice. But that didn't make it difficult. She *did* want to trust the man. This no longer was inexplicable or embarrassing to her. It now felt natural.

If the shadows weren't worth worrying about she wouldn't worry about them. But to be safe, she decided to stick close to Rake and clutched his arm tightly. He seemed to be lost in thought. Was he preparing another long speech? Beth wasn't sure which she liked less: his terse, uninformative replies or his occasional disquisition. What she liked least was never knowing which to expect.

"Each of us can only comprehend the small, specific world around our person," Rake explained, turning and looking down at her curled form on his arm.

Didn't that strain his neck? It would serve him right. If he wanted to talk to her, he should lower his head toward hers. Who knew what could happen then?

"We can read of more but cannot experience it," he continued, failing to make any such accommodation.

Beth responded with a pronounced pout.

"We learn to navigate our little world as best we can. That is our purpose, and we spend many years accomplishing it. Each individual is a finely-tuned machine, ideally adapted to their environment and no other."

"We can travel to expand our horizons," Beth observed.

"Even the well-traveled truly bind themselves to only a few small localities in time and place. These are the worlds they have learned to be part of, the worlds which accept them."

Beth wondered why she hesitated to ask Rake directly about the shadows and creaks. For some reason, she felt it would be ... indelicate. When had *that* ever stopped her before? If he was reluctant to speak of them himself, there must be a reason. Did she really want to know that reason? They had stopped moving. She looked up, and Rake was staring down at her.

"What happens when the world someone knows changes or vanishes?" he put to her.

"The world is always changing."

"True, but ordinarily it does so slowly and in

small ways. We can keep up, for a time."

Beth shrugged. "We adapt."

Rake shook his head. "A person cannot truly adapt. They will opine for the world they once knew and will be lost in the one they find themselves in. Maybe they can survive, but it will be a struggle. It will not be *their* world, and they will not be at home in it."

"What does any of this have to do with immortality?"

"If you were immortal, the world would outpace you again and again. You would be bound to a specific time and place, but you would outlive it. Once your world has receded too far into the distance, you will find yourself in an endless succession of strange lands. Any progress you make toward understanding one will be washed away by the next. You will be alone and adrift, forever. The world will move on, but you will not."

"That can happen if you are mortal too."

"And it does. But it is less likely to happen quickly enough. Before your home can vanish, you have children. Your purpose then is to raise them, and they will be bound to the new world in your stead. By the time the world leaves you behind, there remains no *you* to leave behind."

"I see, so that's what you mean."

Rake nodded. "Mortality is the way we begin anew."

Beth felt a pang of regret. "*If* you have children."

"No. Children are the way life begins anew, but it does not matter whose they are. Whether yours or not, they are not you. Death is death, and others are others. That they share the same name means nothing."

"Then what are you saying? What is the point of mortality if you don't have children?"

"There is no point to it. It simply is. This is the reason it must be, not the reason it is."

Beth groaned, but then smiled.

"So by that token, *your* world is long gone." She realized how cruel this must sound before it even left her mouth. Had he upset her that much? She had made the choice not to have children or, more precisely, had not made the choice to have them. She couldn't blame him for that. Nonetheless, it was irritating.

Rake walked on and said nothing. She could not see his face from behind.

"It must be very lonely," Beth added some time later, well aware that this too was cruel. Was she perversely trying to evoke suffering so she could console him? She was dismayed at the thought but could not discount this possibility. How could she not know her own purpose? Beth resolved to watch her words more vigilantly. If she cared for Rake, she would not allow herself to hurt him.

"Why?" he asked.

"With nobody else down here?"

"I told you, there are others down here."

"You said they are not sociable. If so, you are alone."

"*You* are here."

This reply troubled and annoyed and pleased Beth, though she suspected it was nothing more than a polite evasion.

"That's not what I mean," she grumbled.

Rake turned and faced her. "To be lonely requires time and the sense of its span. Here, there only are places. Walking effaces all sorrows."

Was this hidden world a narcotic? The last refuge of the desperate? Beth wondered whether this meant she was one of the desperate who required refuge. How many other refuges must she have exhausted before finding herself at the last one?

Perhaps the whole thing was in her mind. Was she really gibbering away in a padded cell somewhere? Beth brushed aside that thought, or so she hoped. She really felt as if something had brushed it aside for her. A gentle hand dabbing at tears that never were. She looked up, but Rake was out of reach.

"Is that why you came here?" she asked. "To forget?"

"I do not think so. If I did, it worked."

Beth felt a growing suspicion. If this place was a narcotic, whose narcotic was it?

"Who built this place?" she asked.

"Nobody built it. I told you, it is the echo of things above."

"How do you know that?" Come to think of it, how did he know *anything*? He seemed so confident at times, even if he caveated and qualified everything, and even if half of what he said was incomprehensible guru-talk. But where did he learn it? Were there books down here? Maybe someone had taught him.

"I know nothing with certainty," he replied.

"That can be taken two ways."

Rake grinned. "Both true but without certainty."

"The places you visit — how do you know they exist before you get there?"

"I could not get there if they did not."

Beth shook her head. "That's not what I mean. How do you know they actually are there when you are not?"

"How do you? Could not the same be said of anything anywhere?"

"There is a world to tell me, to broadcast and record and forecast their existence."

"But all that you know passes through the same gatekeepers. Your eyes, your ears, your tongue."

Something about the way he lingered on each word was tantalizing.

"Nonetheless, the evidence is more substantial," she objected. "It would take a lot to keep things consistent, to recreate the world I expect when I expect it."

"Not if you were recreated in its stead."

She was not entirely sure what he meant by this but did not ask. Doing so would risk a digression, and she wanted to suss out where he had learned about the place.

"If the tunnels opened before me," he continued, "they would close behind me. I could not sustain such a grand vision alone."

"Maybe you do not. Maybe it is the vision of the people above."

"Then it would change."

"True, but it could be filtered through you."

Rake stopped and rubbed his chin. "I remember thinking something similar once."

"What did you conclude?"

"That this world is as real as the one above and quite independent of me."

"But when we entered that one room, it was as I saw the world," Beth replied. "You said so."

"True, but it could take time for the world above to trickle through. Maybe that was a place where the membrane separating the two was thinner."

"Then why didn't you see such rooms without me? They still should trickle through."

Rake thought about this for a while. "How long has the world been different from this?"

"A long time."

He seemed surprised. "I did not think it had been so long. How long, if you do not mind my asking?"

This was something Beth had been wondering as well. The trappings varied a lot, and it was difficult to place their era. Nor was she an expert on all things historic. An antiquarian probably would know, matching specific things with late this era or early that era.

"If I had to guess, half a century," she answered at length. "Perhaps longer. Some things feel much older."

"Feel?"

Beth shrugged. "I don't know exactly what they are supposed to look like. Maybe they are older, but I'm not sure."

Rake pondered this. "What is the oldest thing you have seen here?"

Beth stifled the urge to joke that it was him. She had a difficult time recalling, which hardly came as a surprise given how unobservant she had been most of the time. Everything looked generically similar after a while, and she had tired of trying to remember what each room held.

She scrunched up her face and thought back. "Probably those ruins we saw earlier. Also, that broken stone pillar and empty tub."

Rake considered this. "I see. Then I do not know the answer."

"The answer?"

"To whether the world above trickled through before you were here. Maybe the trickling needs a focus. A piece of the world above down below. Some sort of catalyst."

"So we *do* create this world."

"You can call it what you wish, but to say we create something sounds grandiose. A filament does not create light. It merely carries the electricity. Perhaps we are the seeds from which change grows, but it does not transpire by our will. Our volition does not create it, but our memories can guide it."

"*That* seems grandiose. I'm a person, like any other." Beth gave a mischievous grin. "Aside from my devilish beauty, of course. A person is a person, regardless of the world they live in."

"Not so. As I said, you are bound to the world you grew up in. You have formed a contract with it. That is what keeps you from adapting to other worlds. Your home is that world, and it is indelibly imprinted upon you. In this way, you contain the world above you, are a piece of it, and bear its essence."

"And that's enough?"

"I do not know. Perhaps it may draw the rest of

that world down, slowly and imperfectly."

Beth looked at Rake. "That means you *aren't* a suitable catalyst for the current world. Despite the way you speak, you don't seem that old."

"To you."

"What about to *you*?"

"I told you: we are protected from change. But that does not mean we are immune to the passage of time. I still perceive it, though maybe not in the same way."

"Were you alone the whole time?" Beth felt a terrible sadness. What must that have been like? Centuries alone in the dead silence of this place.

Rake turned away and seemed to be struggling with something. A few moments later, his face returned to its usual inscrutable expression. "I think I used to be lonely sometimes. But that changed. Perhaps I grew accustomed to this place, or it to me."

Beth suddenly felt terrible. How could she be so insensitive? When her brief sojourn with him came to an end, she would leave and return to her life above — but Rake would be consigned back to unrelenting solitude. Would she really be able to do that to him?

Maybe that was why she never saw him sleep. Perhaps he passed the long decades between asleep, and then relished every moment of companionship while awake. If so, why hadn't *she* slept? Something didn't add up. Maybe the spell which kept her anxiety at bay also alleviated his loneliness. It was quite possible that this place had different effects on different people. Rake himself had hinted as much.

Was that why he seemed so detached? It stood to reason that the sort of spell which prevented loneliness would dampen his feelings for others. Perhaps if she overcame this, he wouldn't *need* to suppress his feelings for her. But wouldn't that be cruel? If she disabled the spell and then left, he truly would be damned. She imagined how *she* would feel if he broke *her* spell and abandoned her, alone in the dark with no leash on her terror.

Beth desperately wanted to ask why he had forsaken his previous life above and whether it had been voluntary, but that potentially could evoke some painful history. He did not seem to have fond memories of the world above. She wished to cure his pain, not compound it. While they were together, she would do all she could for the man. *Were* they together? She never had been clear on this point. No, she wouldn't make this about her. She had to divert the conversation — but not too far afield, or she would draw obvious attention to her blunder and aggravate any harm.

"So you are as old as the things down here?" Beth asked, her voice artificially chipper.

Rake considered this. "I do not know. Maybe older. It is possible that these things are from when I stopped adapting. That could have been the last time I went above before this. I do not remember."

Beth looked at him closely.

"So, all this will change if I stay here?" She *had* made it all about her. Well, if she wished to distract Rake from the imminent prospect of her departure, it wasn't a bad way.

"If you stay here," — Rake seemed lost in

thought for a moment, then looked at her— "other things may change too."

"But what about you? You're still down here."

"If I vanish tomorrow, this place will not change or disappear. But perhaps the percolation will be quicker. I do not think I repel the world above. I simply am not of it, at least in its current form. However, it is quite possible that, as a residue of an older world, I keep it at bay."

Residue? That struck Beth as a degrading way to describe himself. Did Rake really view himself as residue? Maybe he had been so quiet and aloof because he was depressed. This possibility hadn't occurred to her before but suddenly seemed quite real. If he *was* depressed, that would explain a lot. Did this place reflect his mood?

Notwithstanding his thesis about immortality, Beth doubted Rake *was* bound to a particular time and place. The things she had seen were too varied. However, it was possible that he had stopped adapting at some point. Maybe he got tired of doing so, or maybe he regarded the world above as no longer worth adapting to.

If he dragged this place with him, then, just as he had posited, its apparent era would be around the time he stopped adapting. That meant Rake could be a lot older than he seemed. Intriguing as this was, Beth realized she was focusing on the wrong end of the timeline. If what he said about the place was true, why did it seem tied to *any* era.

"Then why is there nothing *really* old down here?" Beth asked.

"I do not follow your meaning."

"Why are there no ancient rooms? Even the ruin I mentioned wasn't *that* old." Beth was uncertain how she knew this, but she somehow did. She was no expert but liked to think she was experienced enough to tell a real ruin from a knock-off. Ancient ruins inspired a certain reverence, and she didn't feel it here.

"I've wondered about that myself," Rake confessed. "I think it is because this land used to be sparsely inhabited."

"But there were natives. What about their version of this place?"

Rake shrugged. "Maybe their below vanished when they did, replaced with what you see now." He thought for a few moments. "I don't think it ever was like this, though. Much as the land's original inhabitants were scattered and few, this place, if it existed, probably consisted of a few isolated pockets. If the people above were nomadic, the world below would have no way to reflect that. Perhaps it never formed at all. That is the most likely explanation."

"But that doesn't explain why all the stuff here is from within the last century. There were plenty of people and places above during the century or two before this."

"True."

"Then, where is their stuff?"

"I do not know," Rake replied.

Beth couldn't tell whether she had found a true lacuna in Rake's knowledge or he had decided this was an easy way to deflect her questions, another version of "I do not remember." She vaguely recalled one of her sister's boyfriends doing something similar.

Sister? This time it took several minutes to remember who that was, but Beth no longer let that bother her. By now it was clear that the memories weren't gone; they just had been filed for storage, pushed from the fore by the rush of new information. This was understandable to her. Any person finding themselves in a new world would have trouble assigning immediacy to the components of their old one.

Did that mean the missing pieces of Rake's memory weren't truly gone either? Maybe he wasn't looking hard enough. Beth wondered if she could inspire him to recollect them. The idea of being his inspiration pleased her, but she wasn't sure she wanted to compete with those memories. Who knew what sort of longing they could evoke? Perhaps there was a reason he wasn't looking. Maybe all he needed to remember was that he didn't need to remember. Was the same thing happening to her? She felt that pushing her sister into cold storage should bother her a lot more than it did.

What *did* bother Beth was that it was an unequal exchange. Any new understanding paled next to what she had lost. The details of this place were easy to grasp, but the whole eluded her. Its *purpose* eluded her. That was not true up above. There, she easily could assign purpose to things, place, and self. Here, she had no purpose.

Beth doubted she could make this place hers and truly own its essence without such an understanding. This reasoning puzzled her as well. What sort of nonsense was she espousing? Why would she want to 'own its essence,' whatever that meant? She tried to recapture the idea that had motivated this, but found it difficult to concentrate. Was this also a quality of the place — to addle her brain? She was perpetually on the edge of an epiphany that never came.

Once more, Beth forced herself to focus. Essence, storage, sister, sister's boyfriend. She had found her way back. But what *about* her sister's boyfriend? He had done something. Right. He had a way of zoning out when he was being pestered. He'd keep replying 'not sure' and 'don't know.' She had gone through all these mental gymnastics to remember *that*? The idiot was incomparable to Rake in any way. It almost felt like an insult to mention the two in the same sentence.

Beth groaned and wondered what was happening to her. Why did her sister put up with being brushed off that way? Maybe she just wanted to know he was there. She probably would have been as happy with a placebo boyfriend who made soft beeping noises.

Beth remembered that there was a reason for this train of thought. She wondered how the boyfriend would have reacted if her sister pressed the point and demanded his attention? Their mother had that bad habit. She began each sentence with 'Beth', and waited until acknowledged before continuing. She also frequently paused, watching Beth's face until a nod or grunt or some other sign of engagement was forthcoming. Sometimes, she insisted on a full verbal response. That was particularly tiring. Beth never could relax around her mother. The engine always had to be on.

What would have happened if her sister had tried that with her boyfriend? A fight? A breakup? Success? But Rake was different. Beth wasn't sure she wanted success if it came at the price of making herself odious to him. Was that what her mother was to her? Odious? Beth felt ashamed and terribly sorry. Her mother was anything but odious. Probably. It was hard to remember.

Beth once again decided not to question Rake's memory or intentions. If he had consigned something to oblivion, she would respect that. And if he wished to brush her off, she would not make a nuisance of herself. But that didn't mean she would remain silent.

"Perhaps it took this form because you discovered it," Beth said. "Or created it."

Rake looked at her. "You seem enamored of that word, so I will not trouble to correct it."

Was he chiding or rebuking her? Beth recognized a new danger. Even if he didn't brush her off with 'uh huh' or 'not sure', this could be worse. She had seen a coworker do something similar when dealing with a contentious client. Eventually, the woman gave up trying to advise him and simply acknowledged whatever he said without agreeing or disagreeing. The client had 'won' by turning his attorney into an expensive block of wood.

Beth liked this tactic but lacked the disposition to pull it off. Worse, she always had been afraid of driving others to use it on *her*. She didn't want to be the sort of person who 'drove' others to anything. She wanted to convince people, not wear them down. Beth didn't sense that Rake was there yet, but she very well could be on that path with him.

"Putting that aside, *could* you have discovered the place?" she asked. "Maybe it's this way because you were the first inhabitant."

"My memory does not go back that far."

"You mean it was before your time?"

"No, but my memory does not go back that far. It fades quickly when it comes to such things. They probably are not important."

So his memory really *was* porous. He had said something to that effect before — and how this may be a blessing — but that was in regard to being above. Down here, she doubted that he required any such defense. Perhaps it had to do with his age. If he *was* that old, it stood to reason that new memories would crowd out the old. On the other hand, it could be psychological. Or a complete fabrication.

Beth prayed it was psychological. If his memories truly were gone, the same could happen to her. Would her sister actually vanish? She had heard somebody describe dementia this way. Normally, a memory was there even if it was hard to locate, but with dementia it was truly gone and no amount of effort could recover it.

Deprioritizing her sister was bad enough, but forgetting her would be unbearable. Would Beth know what she had lost? Maybe that was what made it tolerable for Rake. What about her mother? Beth once again quashed such thoughts. She realized she had been quashing thoughts a lot lately.

"But you *could* have been the first one down here," she insisted. "All of this could be here because of you. You seemed pretty certain it was not, but I don't think you should be."

"It is possible," Rake replied after some time. Beth was unsure whether he had been trying to remember or was thinking about something else altogether or perhaps nothing at all.

"Maybe there used to be others here with me but I alone remain," he added.

Beth suddenly had an idea. "Could those above actually have started down here? Perhaps we're looking at the whole thing upside down."

Rake shook his head. "I do not think one can conceive a child down here."

Well, that could be good news. When something *did* develop with Rake, she wouldn't need to worry about birth control.

Beth turned red. For some reason, whatever romance she envisioned never had explicitly included *that*. What would it be like, she wondered? He didn't seem like the most adventurous lover. Maybe he never had been one. On the other hand, he never refused her anything — even if he did evade most of her questions. Maybe she needed to take *him* on an adventure. She could lead the way when it came to this. Well, for now she would just try to loosen him up a bit.

"Don't you want to know?" she grinned, clutching his arm.

"Whether I know or not won't alter the fact. Only the here and now matters, not where it came from."

Beth rolled her eyes and dropped his arm. Why had she expected anything more? Wasn't that the definition of madness: trying the same thing over and over and expecting different results? She surveyed the room they found themselves in. Well, down here it could work. Each space was different, and who knew what possibilities it could bring?

They spent the rest of the day in silence. Beth had nothing to say, and Rake said nothing.

―•―

The silence extended into the morning and afternoon of the next day, punctuated only by an occasional practical remark. It wasn't an awkward silence or an angry silence or a contemplative silence. It wasn't the depressing silence of an old bookshop nobody visited or the peaceful silence of a mountaintop. It just was silence. Beth actually enjoyed it. She found it soothing. Rake had a pleasant voice and never grew angry, but the quiet was even more comforting. It let her mind rest. The silence was not *of* the place, it *was* the place.

Without thinking, she broke it.

"Are you are trying to find a replacement?" she asked.

Rake stopped. For a moment, Beth worried that she had made an irrevocable blunder. Perhaps he had been weaving the silence for her, drawing her in. Now, she had shattered it. A cellphone in a concert, a screaming baby in a library. The elegant tapestry was torn, never to be mended. It would be easier to burn the shreds and start over.

"A replacement for yourself," she clarified.

"Why would I need a replacement?"

Beth shrugged. "Maybe you're tired of being down here as caretaker or whatever."

Rake raised an eyebrow. "I am not a caretaker."

"Maybe your time is drawing near."

"Time for what?"

Beth realized with horror that she had been on autopilot. Was she teasing him about death? What if he *was* nearing his end? That would be terribly callous of her.

"Time to leave." It was the best recovery she could manage.

"I can leave whenever I desire to."

Beth sighed in exasperation. "Time to die."

"How would I know when it is my time to die? Nobody knows such a thing, unless they intend to make it happen."

"Do you?" She spoke slowly, as if to a mentally unstable client.

"I have no reason to die, and I am not tired of being here."

Beth was very attentive to his tone. There was no irritation in it, though the words easily could have been construed that way.

"I'm sorry," she offered.

To her surprise, Rake smiled. "There is no need to apologize. You wish to know what will become of you."

"Become of me?" His wording troubled Beth. "Aren't you guiding me to my mother's place?"

"You need not worry. I have no power over you. What becomes of you is entirely up to you."

"But we *are* going to my mother's place, right?"

"It is impossible to replace someone. A new person in place of the old is not a replacement. It is a new person."

Beth was not exactly scared, but she found his refusal to confirm this particular point a bit unsettling. After a few minutes passed, she no longer could contain herself. She stopped and called Rake's name. If doing that worked for her mom, it could work for her. She was willing to risk annoying the man.

"Rake, where are you leading me?" she demanded.

He seemed confused. "I am not leading you anywhere."

Beth felt dizzy, but quickly recovered. "What about my mother's place?"

"I'm accompanying you there, not leading you."

Beth faced him, hands on hips and one hundred percent frustration. "I fail to see the distinction."

"You felt it was demeaning to be led, so we are walking together," Rake quietly explained.

Beth vaguely recalled something to that effect, and her temper subsided a bit.

"God you're pedantic. Why can't you be straightforward?"

"What one person finds straightforward, another finds circuitous."

"There. THERE. Like THAT. Is that necessary?"

"We will get there whether we speak or no. If you find my speech bothersome, would you prefer I not say anything?"

This did not feel like a threat or challenge, though from anyone else it would have. Beth sighed. It was just Rake being Rake.

She took his hand and replied softly, "No, that would make me sad."

He said nothing, so she struggled to find a new line of inquiry. If she peppered him with questions, things would return to normal. What was it she needed from him, though? Unable to think of anything specific, she asked the first thing that popped into her head.

"You said you have led others."

"Indeed."

"But you're not leading me."

"You're the first to walk alongside me. Or maybe the first in a long time."

She wished he would make up his mind on that point. It didn't really matter, but she would feel better if she were the first. She truly *would* be special.

"And there were others too. Ones who ended up here without you."

Rake nodded.

"And they left."

He was about to reply, when she corrected herself. She did not wish to get drawn into a rehash of *that* fruitless discussion.

"Some left, and you don't know what became of the others. Does that pretty much sum it up?"

"That is correct."

"So my point is that some people who were down here returned to the surface. Like we're doing." She placed an emphasis on this last bit.

Rake nodded.

"Then why does nobody above know about this place? Wouldn't someone have reported it?" The possibilities Beth had considered earlier struck her as plausible enough, but it still was a good question. Most important, it was *a* question and would keep the conversation alive.

"That, I do not know. I cannot say what those I led did after I led them. I expect some were happy and some were not. Maybe they wanted to find their way back but could not."

"I'm talking about the ones who managed to leave."

Rake stopped and turned toward her. "As am I. Just because they left this place does not mean it left them. They found their way back to the surface, but perhaps not to themselves."

Beth stared at him. What did *that* mean? Was it a disclaimer of some sort? Maybe he was warning her not to be disappointed when things didn't turn out as she hoped.

"That doesn't explain why nobody above has heard of this place."

Rake shrugged. "If they were not the same when they returned, the above may have rejected them. Maybe they tried to return here or hid in some dark corner of the above, desperately pretending it was the below. As I said, some may be happy and some may not."

"But *somebody* would have said *something*. It sounds like there were more than a few, and you said some may have been happy when they got home. Even the ones who regretted leaving — wouldn't they have shared the story of what they lost? Or maybe attempted to recreate it up above?"

"Perhaps it is a story they did not wish to tell. Or maybe they tried. Not every story finds an ear. It is quiet down here, but the noise above is constant and loud. It can be very difficult to hear a particular story there, or to discern what is worth hearing."

Beth pondered this for a while.

"I think I know what this place is," she eventually announced.

"I once thought the same," Rake replied.

"I think it was brought into existence by you."

Rake smiled at her. "You have expressed this sentiment quite often. Let us reason it through. If that is true, what does it say about you? You are now in this place and thus part of it."

Beth stopped in her tracks. She did not like the sound of that one bit.

"Do not let this disturb you," Rake reassured her. "When you are in the above, you are part of that. When you are in the below, you are part of this."

"And you? Are you part of the above when you go there?"

"No. I feel no affinity for it and am as uninvited there as those who stumble into this place are here."

"So I am a part of it because I was invited?"

Rake's eyes wandered over her. "Indeed. Do not think this is a bad thing. It imposes no obligation, and you can refuse the invitation if you so desire. I feel no affinity for the above, so I am never part of it. If you feel an affinity for it, you will be."

Beth grinned. "And does the below feel an affinity for *me*?"

"It does. You would not have been invited otherwise."

Was this his roundabout way of saying he liked her? Would she actually get an answer from him if she pressed the matter?

"If I'm part of the below, then what part am I?"

she asked, wrapping herself around Rake's arm and looking up at him.

Rake nodded. "That is a wise question to ask. The manner of your entry to a place makes all the difference. Queen and servant both are part of a kingdom, as is the block on which heads are lost. The difference is the manner in which they were brought into that world."

"And how was I brought into this world?"

"By me," Rake replied. He looked at her. "And by you."

Beth frowned and locked his eyes. "In this place that was made by you, am I a queen or a servant?"

Rake sighed. "As I said, this place really exists. I can move between it and the above, and I can bring things and people" — he took a telling pause — "here and back."

Beth wanted to kick herself. She had slipped up and given him an out. She could have tried to press the matter but decided it was best not to. Forcing a man to tell her what she wanted to hear could only lead to heartbreak. She would relish it all the more when he said the words of his own accord.

Frustrated as she was with her mistake, Beth would not be deterred from her general questioning. She decided to approach things from another angle.

"I don't think it *just* was you," she declared. "Something happened. Something to do with how you first got here."

"And what do you suppose that 'something' was?"

"Something cataclysmic," Beth replied. "Something that shocked the world into creating a place of refuge. You simply happened to be the one to shape that refuge."

Rake's expression was different from any she had seen so far. Was he acknowledging her? He rubbed his chin.

"An intriguing idea. I have no recollection of such a thing, but that does not mean it did not happen. However, the world is not easily shocked. What depravity has it not seen a million times?"

"I'm not talking about a shock to its sensibilities. I mean a physical shock. When someone is about to die, they may not accept it. Maybe they would try to create a safe place away from that intolerable truth."

"And you think the world was about to die and created this place?"

"Exactly."

Rake thought for a few moments. "This place has been here a long time. According to your theory, the world should be dead by now."

Beth shook her head. "Maybe the world operates on a much longer timescale than us."

"The world is not a mind. It is a thing."

"So are we," Beth replied. "If you look closely enough."

"True, but that is different. Though it may possess thinking parts, the world as a whole is not capable of thought. Nor has it the ability create or destroy. It just is."

"How do you know? You said you know nothing with certainty."

Rake smiled. "Your tactics are growing subtler."

"My tactics?"

"All speech is tactics. It is how we probe and

change things. *That* is the medium of creation."

Beth found this a little disturbing. Was all the guru-talk some sort of devious psychological game? She refused to believe that. If there was subtlety, it felt benign.

'Thanks' was all she could muster. She hoped such a tepid response would disarm his two-edged compliment.

Rake gave the slightest nod. "I wonder if I too was someone else once."

"What do you mean?"

"I think you touched on half a truth earlier."

"Which half?" Beth joked, still worried by his implicit accusation. *Was* she employing 'tactics' against him? Was she really that bad? She didn't want to think she was engaged in an ongoing verbal contest with the man.

"We do not change this place to our taste, but perhaps this place changes us."

Beth faked a gasp. "So, I will become you?"

"Why so distraught at the idea? You see me as beautiful. Who in the world above would not wish to be beautiful?"

"I want to be me," Beth protested, suddenly feeling childish. She envisioned herself pounding her chest and scrunching her face. She also cringed at the implication — intended or not — that she wasn't already beautiful. She wouldn't claim to be as beautiful as *him* but liked to imagine she had her own charm.

"And so you are. At least to the extent anyone legitimately can use the word 'me'."

"I won't be if I change."

"Change is the nature of life. Without change, we are merely things. Change endows us with being."

Beth looked at him. "So you said. But you also said we are safe from change down here. That would mean we have no being."

Rake smiled. "Being safe from something does not mean it cannot occur. You are safe from the need to eat, but that does not mean you cannot eat. Or will not."

Beth had not tried eating but sensed no impediment to it. Would she then need to use the restroom? Maybe this place would offer every gourmand's dream: the freedom to eat without constraint or consequence. She had no intention of finding out. Not that the opportunity had presented itself; she had yet to come across anything edible. She wondered whether that would change if she truly wished it to.

"I can choose not to eat," she replied.

"Indeed, and you can also choose not to refuse change."

Beth thought about this. "I have not made any choice, or been given one."

"You are constantly being given one and constantly making one. You just do not know it."

"And what makes you think I am allowing change?"

"You are allowing some change but perhaps not all. If you were the type to refuse all change, you would not have been invited here."

Beth groaned. "You say that about everything, and it sounds like a cop-out. If I do something it is inevitable because I would not have been invited if I weren't the type to do it."

"Quite right. At least when it comes to certain things, and this is one of them. But you need not fret over it. You'll always be 'me', but what you call 'me' may change."

Beth sighed. "I'm not sure which I find more disturbing."

"That too will change."

"How so?"

"You will be sure."

⁓•⁓

The first time it happened was terrifying. Beth had been lost in thought after spotting a record player almost identical to her childhood one. When she finally looked up, she was alone in a long hallway with rows of doors on either side.

She felt a wave of nausea and wondered what could come up since she hadn't eaten in weeks. In this place, she'd probably spew random objects. Old hammers and bedsheets and maybe a bronze chandelier. Bronze chandelier? She looked up and there was one on the ceiling. Was that where the idea had come from?

Beth struggled to keep her wits about her. She hadn't spaced out for that long, so Rake had to be nearby. She called out, but there was no reply. To her surprise, there also was no echo. Had that always been the case? She didn't notice its absence before but hadn't been paying attention. Or maybe this particular room was designed to dampen sound. That would make sense in a hotel, which is what she assumed this was meant to be.

She tried to remember the rules for being lost in a forest. The first was don't *get* lost. Wasn't she supposed to follow the left wall? No, that was for a labyrinth. Here, the left wall would lead her in circles around the room.

Spiraling outward wouldn't work either. This wasn't a forest, so why did she expect forest rules to help? The only strategy that made sense was to remain in place until somebody found her. However, this assumed somebody was searching for Beth. Would Rake notice she was gone? If he did, he probably would assume she'd have no trouble finding her way back to him. He was convinced she could, so why bother searching for her?

Perhaps this was a test. It couldn't be mere coincidence that she found herself in the quintessential 'pick a door' movie setup. Or was it a game show? What's behind door number eighteen? Probably the same as what was behind all the others: darkness and despair.

Beth took a deep breath. There was light, but she couldn't assume it would last. Maybe once Rake got far enough away it would fade and vanish. She had to act before that happened. At least it showed no signs of dimming for now. Perhaps he was waiting behind one of the doors, and she was meant to figure out which one. There only were twenty possibilities.

She closed her eyes and tried to sense which door it was. Nothing. Beth was ashamed that she had imagined such nonsense would work. She plunked herself down on the carpet. Even if it *was* for the forest, staying in place was the only strategy she had. The best way to be found was not to get more lost.

After what seemed like an hour or two, Beth rose. She had to accept reality, and she had to do it sooner rather than later. Rake probably wasn't trying to find her. He had hinted that he could find things down here, so presumably he *could* find her — if he cared to. Obviously, he did not. It would be bad enough if he was just waiting, but the man probably hadn't even stopped walking.

This lent additional urgency to her situation. If Rake *hadn't* stopped, he would become more and more difficult to catch up with. He didn't walk very fast, at least when they were together, but he rarely tarried of his own accord. The distance between them could quickly become insurmountable if she made a single mistake, like sitting there for a couple of hours.

Beth grappled with a volatile cocktail of anger and hurt. Rake had promised to lead her out, and this felt like a betrayal. She wished she could remember the precise wording of his promise. Such details made all the difference. She knew this from her work. A single word too many or too few could be the difference between penury and wealth, freedom and incarceration, happiness and despair.

Was she being unfair to him? Maybe Rake was frantically looking for her but simply hadn't succeeded yet. She couldn't imagine him *frantically* doing anything, but that didn't mean he had abandoned her. He said he could find things here, not that it would be easy.

Beth wondered why she wasn't panicking.

Despite her initial shock, the gravity of the situation didn't weigh on her. In fact, she felt like sitting down again. Even if he never came, and she was stuck there forever, things somehow would work out. She was reminded of what she had read about hypothermia. A sense of well-being, then sleepiness, then death. At least she wasn't sleepy. Mustering her resolve, Beth decided to take action.

There was a room and there were doors. She would test Rake's assertion. If she had the inexplicable ability to find her way out, then by some miracle she would pick the right door. Or maybe it would *become* the right door once she picked it. The way out? Was that what she was looking for, or did she want to find Rake? If she could navigate her own way out, would she be willing to do so alone?

That certainly would avoid an awkward introduction to her mother or a more awkward refusal to make one. Perhaps this was his way of being considerate. Had he realized her conundrum and decided to leave right before the exit?

The thought made her sadder than she could have imagined. For the first time since following him in, Beth felt like crying. At the very least, she would have liked to say goodbye. She quietly had harbored the hope she wouldn't have to. Her eyes grew cold. No, if he was being considerate he would have left her in a place with a single, obvious exit. Maybe a goodbye was *just* what she needed.

If she remembered the film trope correctly, the door at the end always held the monster. She considered opening all the other doors first but decided against it. That would make her feel too exposed. A single door meant a single path and a single threat from whatever was behind it. If only one door led to safety, she would be a fool to open them all.

Beth was standing before an open door. It was the fifth from the end on the right. She did not remember opening it, but her hand was on the doorknob. Her body must have made the decision that her mind refused. Maybe it didn't matter *which* door she chose, as long as she chose one. Or maybe she had made a conscious decision but abdicated the memory of it. Her confusion drove home just how difficult the measure of time was in this place. For all she knew, she already had tried every other door.

The space beyond the door was unremarkable, no different from myriad others she had passed through with Rake. The only thing missing was him.

Steeling herself, Beth stepped through the door. She closed and reopened it. The long hall was still there and still lit. With an air of resignation, she closed the door again and crossed the new room. It had two exits and she picked one.

~•~

When Beth finally found Rake, she cried. She couldn't tell whether it had been days or weeks or months. She rushed up to him and hugged him tightly. He smiled but did not seem surprised. Her relief turned to anger, and she felt like slapping him.

"You idiot," she sobbed. "Why did you leave me there?"

"Leave you where?"

Was it possible that he *hadn't* noticed she was gone? Was Rake an automaton, engaging with those he came across and nothing more?

"You promised you wouldn't abandon me!" Beth screamed.

He dabbed away her tears. "I did not abandon you. You are here and I am here."

"That's not what I mean. You didn't stop when I fell behind."

"Did you need me to?"

Beth was about to lash out at him but realized he was right. *Did* she need him to?

"You said you hardly ever see others," she quietly complained. "I could have been lost forever."

"I also said that you are different. You can find the way."

"You didn't *know* that," she fumed, her voice rising again. "Listen, I put up with a lot of your bullshit. Your guru-talk is all well and good when it's just talk. But if you abandon me, I really can get lost and I really can die." *Die*. She hadn't truly considered this until now. She *could* die down here. It was a real possibility.

"I think I understand," Rake replied.

Beth's jaw dropped. Had her unadorned fury actually penetrated that thick skull of his?

"Stray-talk."

"What?"

Rake smiled. "I promised I would name your manner of speech."

"That's not what I ..."

"I speak as I walk and think, along a single unwavering path," Rake continued. "But it seems this is not your way. You think and talk in a sinuous fashion."

Beth pouted. "Well, that's rather insulting." She had not expected him to remember, but *this*? It was no better than being called a ditz. She would have preferred something dignified with a hint of femininity, though she had no idea what.

"It is not intended that way," Rake explained.

"I don't care how you damned-well meant it," Beth growled. "You don't know a thing about how I think."

Rake grinned. "You are mistaken. I have been listening to it for a while now."

"You can hear what I think!?!!" It wasn't the most wildly implausible claim he had made. She wondered whether that was her new yardstick for sanity.

"Of course."

"Why didn't you say something?" Beth demanded, hands on hips. If he could read her thoughts, he knew how she felt about him — which meant his indifference was just that. He wasn't oblivious to her feelings, he simply didn't requite them.

"I thought it was obvious since you do the same," he replied.

Her arms relaxed. Could he *actually* read thoughts, or was this another vertiginous exercise in sophistry? That she gave any credence to the idea worried Beth.

"How so?"

"I say what I mean, therefore you know what I think. Do you not say what you mean?"

Beth almost laughed. The man had her. She wanted to be angry but instead felt relieved. If he merely was oblivious, that left some hope.

"Stray-talk?" she repeated with a raised eyebrow. "That's hardly flattering."

"Flattery is pointless. Would you prefer I lie to you?"

Beth once again wanted to hit the guy, but she sighed instead. "Let me get back to you on that."

Rake smiled. "You do not."

"No, I suppose not." There was a moping quality to her voice, and she struggled to recover her composure.

"However, I also prefer that you don't leave me behind."

"I did not leave you behind. I accommodated your style."

He was beginning to sound a lot like a boyfriend explaining why he hadn't really cheated. Beth eyed him skeptically.

"Your speech and thought is stray-talk," Rake continued. "So it follows that your path must involve stray-walk."

"And what does this stray-walk entail, might I inquire?" Beth asked through gritted teeth.

"Exactly what it sounds like. You are peripatetic. Rather than taking the shortest path from A to B, you meander. Perhaps your path crosses itself at times."

Beth groaned. "Okay, I get it, I get it. I have no sense of direction." She glared at him. "That doesn't justify abandoning me."

"You misunderstand. I am not criticizing your manner of walking. One way is not better than another. If your style does not contradict your desire, then there is nothing wrong with it."

"Well, it contradicted my desire not to get lost. And my desire for *you* not to lose me."

Rake put his hand on her head. She wasn't sure whether this was meant as comfort or condescension. All she knew was that she didn't dislike it.

"I have long perceived your style, though I did not name it until now. Previously, it was confined to speech and thought."

"What do you mean?"

"You were following me, so you had no latitude to exercise your style."

Beth knocked his hand off her head. "I'm *still* following you, dammit. And you're still leading me out. As you promised."

Rake shook his head, and her stomach sank. *Was* he abandoning her? This felt like a breakup.

"You followed me in the beginning, then you walked by my side, and now you have begun to seek your own way."

"I didn't *seek* anything," Beth grumbled. "I got lost."

Rake shook his head.

"You chose your own path."

Beth looked at him. Maybe *he* was the one who felt insecure. Why hadn't she considered that?

"I'm still with you," she replied, unsure exactly what he wanted from her.

"For as long as you want. But you could not have lost me if you did not wish to allow it."

"YOU lost ME," Beth snapped back. "And I certainly did *not* allow it."

"Let me ask you this, then. We have walked in silence for long periods of time before," Rake began.

This *was* a breakup speech. It felt like the old "we've been coasting for a while" line. She felt tears welling up.

"I assume you were not staring at me the whole time," he continued.

"Would it bother you if I was?"

"No," he replied. Beth felt a thrill run down her spine.

"My point," Rake continued, "is that you have been lost in thought frequently and for long periods."

"Is that a crime?"

"If it was, you would have been punished."

Was he flirting with her? It was very hard to tell, but his smirk hinted at something. If so, Beth was too upset to avail herself of it.

"What's your point?" she demanded.

"You never got lost before."

"You never abandoned me before."

"I did nothing different this time," Rake noted. "If you could have gotten lost, you would have many times."

Was he *that* indifferent to her? Perhaps it was mere luck that she had kept up with him for as long as she had.

"That says more about you as a guide than me as a follower," she snapped. "A good guide will slow or stop when needed."

Beth worried that she was letting passion get the better of her. Was she really trying to antagonize the man? Guiding her was a favor, not an obligation. She hadn't hired him, and he never claimed to be skilled at it. Nonetheless, she would not tolerate a complete indifference to her well-being. She realized she had slipped into old modes of thought. 'Complete indifference' was a term she would have used in her professional life above, a life she soon would resume unless he *did* abandon her.

Rake nodded. "When needed."

Beth decided it would not be prudent to continue down this path. She would say something she would regret, maybe even renounce his help. Then she really *would* be screwed. Perhaps that would be the best way to find out if he actually cared about her.

Over the next few days, Beth began to take the lead from time to time, much as Rake had proposed early on. This served two purposes. It restored her sense of equality, something she had relinquished for the majority of their journey. More practically, it also helped prevent a repeat of her previous fiasco. He couldn't leave her behind if she was ahead. If she needed to be guided, he presumably could instruct her from the rear.

Rake did not seem to mind. At times, he advised her with a gentle word or a hand on her shoulder. Beth had assumed he would constantly correct her mistakes, but he did so infrequently. Whether she was good at picking the path or it didn't actually matter was unclear.

She wondered what lay in the places he guided

her away from. Maybe they were places she could not return from, or maybe they ended in nothing or the wrong something. She hadn't asked, and he hadn't answered. He probably would call them 'destinations' and offer up some aphorism cautioning her to stay away from such destinations lest they become her destiny. Beth was quite pleased with herself; that really *did* sound like him.

Over time, she took the lead more and more often. Soon, she exclusively occupied that position. Rake followed quietly and without complaint. He spoke neither more nor less than before, which was not much at all. They had long fallen into a habit of silence, but this just meant she was less talkative. There were many questions, but none Beth cared to ask and which Rake hadn't already answered.

Beth's feelings for Rake had grown stronger since the incident, and she had become no better at articulating them. She doubted he would be receptive, but that didn't curb them. This frustrated her enormously, most of all with herself. His apathy toward her had been made abundantly clear when she was lost, but she couldn't shake the feeling that it wasn't apathy at all. She realized this was wishful thinking. She only had been in a few relationships but knew how easy it was to pretend that what she wanted him to feel was what he actually felt.

At first, she had imagined Rake to be the type of man who would rush to defend her from danger. But according to him, there was no danger to defend her from. The one time she was in peril, he was nowhere to be found. Well, not nowhere. She *had* found him, but through no effort of his own. Of course, she didn't know that for sure. Maybe he was searching for her the whole time and was too proud to admit it, but even she did not believe *that*. No, he thought he was doing the right thing. He wasn't indifferent to her well-being; he genuinely believed there was no danger. What rankled most was that her absence didn't seem to sadden Rake.

This drove home her own feelings about *him*. She had missed him. Terribly. She was much happier now, despite the cloud over their relationship. The mere fact that he was walking silently behind her was enough. She didn't need anything more from him, though she still wanted it. Was this what an old marriage felt like? Two people content to just know the other exists? It could *be* an old marriage. Who knew how many years she had been down there with him?

Beth had finally grown comfortable with the world below. The light was bright everywhere, and each room reminded her of home. She and Rake must have crossed the flyover states of the deep. Now they were back in civilization, or its perverse mirror.

She continued to have long bouts of inattention — when she was completely oblivious to her surroundings — as well as the occasional heated discussion with Rake. Heated on her side, never his. Sometimes she wandered off on her own for a time. This was something she would never have tried before. At least, not voluntarily. The mere thought of being separated from Rake had terrified her until recently. Now she found it liberating. She had started small, remaining within earshot. Then she wandered farther and farther afield. During these strolls, she was quite attentive to her surroundings, carefully recording visual cues to help find her way back to Rake.

For his part, he didn't seem bothered by any of this. She had been very apologetic after her first few forays, but he said nothing. She took this as encouragement. As her side trips grew longer and longer, she was surprised how patient he was. She'd vanish without a word for hours, but he was always waiting when she returned.

One time, the room Beth returned to was different than she remembered it. That was when she realized he *hadn't* been waiting. He had continued his peregrination in her absence. She had no idea how she found her way back to him or why this did not frighten her. From then on, her trips grew longer and bolder. She no longer felt tethered to Rake, confident now that she could always find him when she needed to. If she needed to.

Once, she wandered for what felt like days before reuniting with him. It was unclear who found whom, but they were together again. Beth had no doubt that he always would find her, or she him. She wondered why she didn't miss him during these excursions, as she had when lost that first time. She decided *this* was the difference: she knew he was there. Did it matter whether he was one step or a thousand away? Their paths would always reconnect.

Beth worried about her mother little and infrequently. Her sister no longer entered her thoughts at all. When she did think of her mother, it was as an only child. The triangle had imperceptibly faded into a single edge, and that edge flickered and faded at times. This did not escape her notice, and she wondered whether she always had felt that way. Perhaps the remaining edge was the shadow of a light from above, its substance born of the beliefs and expectations in that place. A bond in more way than one. Beth had no answer.

Did she actually care about her mother at all? She knew that she should. Why was she traveling to see her? There was nothing she could do for the woman. Was it to comfort her mother or vice versa? That would be very selfish of her. Maybe her mother wasn't even alive anymore. Beth had no idea how long she had been down below, and couldn't dismiss the possibility.

Did that mean she would encounter her mother *here*? Rake had said it wasn't that sort of place, and it didn't feel like that sort of place. But that didn't mean it wasn't. She hadn't seen any echoes of people, but maybe Rake had carefully navigated her away from such things. There *had* been the noises and the wobbling and the shadow. Perhaps those were the ones he couldn't avoid. Constrained as they were to the paths, there probably was limited freedom to navigate around such inconveniences.

But why hadn't she run into any on her own? Rake wasn't always with her anymore. Given the number of people above, living and dead, there would be too many echoes anyway. There was no way he could have guided her around most of them. There were many reasons to believe Rake on this point, and none not to.

The prospect of never seeing her mother again

did not bother Beth, though she was confident she would. Rake had promised, and Rake would deliver. But would her mother still be there? Had she ever been there? Part of her didn't want to find out. Down here, she could imagine the woman would live forever, frozen as a fading but never lost memory. There was no reason to contaminate that with the untidiness of an actual dying woman. Did she really need to see Beth? No, that wasn't right. What mother didn't want to see her daughter at the end? But would she be willing for her daughter to sacrifice happiness as the price?

Beth felt terribly ungrateful. She never would have entered this place but for her mother's illness. She owed her for that. She owed her *illness* for that, disgusting as the thought made her feel. Wouldn't her mother want her to find happiness? But in precisely what did such happiness lie? That was the crux of it.

Though she had learned many things — or felt she had or maybe deluded herself into thinking she had — one question had plagued Beth since the beginning. Was it the man or the place? Which did she need and which did she want? It felt as if she and the answer had been flirting at cross purposes this whole time.

Beth did not arrive at the answer or discover it or mature into it. One day, she simply knew it. She had found it or it had found her. It felt like pure serendipity, nothing more. She stopped in her tracks, oblivious to the place around her. The familiar rustling of Rake grew closer, and she waited for him to reach her. This was the epiphany she had been waiting for, and she wanted to share it with him. She turned.

Nobody was there.

This did not feel like the times she had strayed. She always had known Rake was near, even when she feared herself lost. Now she did not know where he was. She remembered Rake saying something similar once, something about not knowing where somebody was in the world. She now knew why he had told her this, why he had told her all the things he had and not told her all the things he had not.

Beth felt sadness but no sorrow. She had what she wanted, what she needed. Maybe they would meet again. Would they recognize one another? Perhaps he would be one of the countless things she passed. She wondered where he was, and if he was anywhere at all.

She looked around and breathed in her world. A prospect once terrifying now felt liberating. She was in the below alone. She knew the light would not fail. If it did, she would grope her way forward. There was too much to explore, too much to know. This world was hers, every inch of it. She saw from afar how childish she had been, fretting about whether she could find her way alone.

She did not need to find her way. She needed to make her way, and this she could do.

◈ THE END ◈

ABOUT THE AUTHOR

K.M. Halpern was born in New York and, after spending far too much time there, finally returned to the Cambridge, MA he knew and loved from graduate school. Unfortunately, all that remained was a large Starbucks, several thousand bank branches, and two small universities whose names he forgets.

He divides his time between ill-considered technical endeavors and ill-considered literary ones. His current projects include a fourth book of very short works (*The Late Worm*), the second novel in *The Tale of Rin* series, a book of pretentious and largely dystopian short stories (*You May Feel a Small Prick*), and a stage-play about a man whose wife vanishes.

K.M. also spends a disturbing amount of time coping with physicsitis, a disease characterized by massive lacunae in one's math knowledge. Oddly enough, for each gap filled three new ones appear. No doubt, this phenomenon easily could be explained through copious hand-waving, a quick and dirty approximation, and a brief, uninformative review of basic math everyone should know but somehow never learned in high school. Unfortunately, K.M. is too busy misunderstanding other areas of math to attend to that.

K.M. holds a PhD in theoretical physics from MIT, more commonly known as 'that odd cluster of concrete buildings on the Charles River.' He may be found at www.kmhalpern.com or generating very small gravitational waves around town.

Milton Keynes UK
Ingram Content Group UK Ltd.
UKHW040834070124
435623UK00002B/3